CURVY BRIDES OF BLOSSOM FORD

BOOKS 1-4

IRIS WEST

Curvy Brides Of Blossom Ford Books 1-4

Copyright 2023 Iris West

All rights reserved.

Would you like a free book? Sign up to my mailing list at http s://dl.bookfunnel.com/t191w45ryj to receive a copy of Loving My Fake Husband, a Curvy Brides of Blossom Ford Series short story and updates on upcoming books, giveaways and more.

MARRYING THE PROTECTIVE PROFESSOR

CURVY BRIDES OF BLOSSOM FORD BOOK 1

IRIS WEST

CHAPTER ONE

August

ALL MY LIFE I'VE secretly wished I was born and raised in an ordinary family, with loving, welcoming parents instead of being the town's sign of bad luck, growing up at Blossom Ford Orphanage and having the town's name as my surname, like the other kids there. I can't help believing if I was wanted, the acceptance and sense of belonging would have helped me become someone who knows how to love. That belief is strongest when I think of Ella Mitchell.

It's Friday night so ensuring she gets home safely is my top priority as I park my SUV a short distance from Jackson's Diner where she's working, far enough to see the door of the restaurant but not so close that anyone might link my presence to the diner. I don't care how the interfering residents of Blossom Ford view me, but I don't want rumors to spread about Ella.

I slide down the car seat, getting comfortable even as I curse myself for the warmth that spreads through my chest at the mere thought of her name. As I've done a millionth time, I tell myself I'm here to protect her.

An uncomfortable tightness in my chest and a bitter taste in my mouth that I'm all too familiar with have me exhaling slowly. But it's hard to chase away the guilt. I cannot keep from committing the same sin. I'm a scarred, divorced, grizzly mountain of a man that's old enough to be her father while she's a beautiful, innocent twenty-two-year-old with her whole life ahead of her. Ella deserves better than me. But I still can't stop thinking about her.

It makes no difference that what I feel for her is more than physical attraction. I love her strength, soft smile and the way she's warm to everyone that crosses paths with her. There's a certainty in my bones that she's meant for me alone. This only makes the guilt worse. I should let her go because I love her.

And I have. To a point. For the last two years since I returned to Blossom Ford, saw her for the first time and fell for the kindness in her honey hued eyes and the sweetest curves I'd ever seen, I've stopped myself from approaching her. From claiming her. At least in real life. Because in my dreams, I've made love to her every single night and spent my days laughing with her. I've always considered my self-control one of my strongest attributes, but I can't stop dreaming about her.

I can't help the fact that I won't have her driving home by herself at midnight, after her shifts at the diner on Fridays and Saturdays. If I'm an asshole, so be it. And if deep down I know as well as ensuring she's safe, I have to see her face, I'll take the guilt and deal with it.

I frown when only two cars remain in the parking lot. One is old Jackson's beat up truck, and the other belongs to Rosie; the woman who works with Ella. Ella's old yellow mini should be right besides Rosie's.

The door to the diner flies open and Rosie marches out in her apron, phone glued to her ear. She sprints to her car. My frown thickens. How is Ella going to get home? Will she be closing on her own? I force myself to stay in the car. As much as I want to rush in and help, keeping a distance is crucial to my self-discipline.

I ramp up the air conditioning in the car a little higher. It usually takes one hour to close, but tonight, it'll take Ella longer. Old Jackson doesn't think hard work hurts women. There's no way he's going to help with setting the diner to the way he likes it.

I keep my eyes on the door and an hour and a half later, I'm rewarded with the sight of Ella's curvy hips wrapped in hugging denim and the soft way her breasts hug her blouse. Even after a ten-hour shift, she's a vision that gets my heart racing.

She zeroes in on my car and it's like she can see me, like she knows I'm waiting here for her. She does this on Fridays and Saturdays; the days I wait for her. If she worked any other nights, I'd wait for her then, too. She's friends with Mrs. Gallagher, the orphanage director who's the closest thing to a mother I've ever had. Ella must think of me as a much older brother who's looking out for her.

She steps on the street and heads towards me. I know that she's just taking the road to her house, but I can't stop my heart from beating even faster. It's like this every time I see her.

I'm feeling something else too; anger. Her walking alone down the empty street at this time of the night is pissing me off.

She's only a few feet from me when a car careens down the street and stops beside her. I sit up straight, hoping a friend is coming to pick her up. But she doesn't slow down, even after spotting the car.

I scowl as a man stumbles out of the car and steps in her path. It's Toby Anderson, Ella's ex. Something ugly rears in me. Despite my unstoppable feelings for Ella, whenever I see him, I realize how great my self-control is. Every time I saw him with Ella, I wanted to knock him out. The four months they dated were an exercise in self-discipline I didn't think I was going to win. But for Ella, to give her the chance at happiness she deserved with someone her age that could give her a comfortable life, I held myself back.

I don't like the way Toby sways on his feet. The light from the full moon and lamppost in front of the diner are enough to make out the disgust on Ella's face. Before I know it, my hand is on the door handle, but my eyes don't stray from Toby.

They are talking but the loud music and shouts from the car stop me from hearing what they are saying. Toby reaches out a hand and touches Ella's arm. She wrenches it back.

I'm out of the car. I sprint towards them, her safety the only thought in my mind. For her, I'd tried staying away, but her safety is something I'll not compromise on. Even if it means she might hate me for interfering with her life.

CHAPTER TWO

Ella

"STAY AWAY FROM ME!" I move back, keeping my eyes on Toby's face even as my hand reaches for the pepper spray inside my bag. The expression in Toby's eyes is creeping me out.

"Bitch," he spits and takes a step toward me.

My hand reaches for the spray, but before I can whisk it out, Toby's hand reaches towards me so fast I close my eyes.

A grunt and surprised shouts reach my ears. When I inch my eyes open, the first thing I see is August Ford, crushing back Toby's arm. The younger man struggles to pull away, but he doesn't stand a chance against August's toned muscles.

Relief floods through me.

"Who the fuck are you?" Toby screams.

"I believe the lady doesn't want to speak with you. I'll let you go if you are ready to get back into your car and drive off."

Toby's face is twisted in pain. One of his friends comes out of the car. And cowers back in when August's eyes arrow in on him.

I'm glad Toby's friends won't gang up against August, who shoves Toby towards his car. Toby stumbles before righting himself. The venom in his eyes as he glares at me has my stomach tightening in knots.

"We're not done."

August stands beside me and puts his arm around my shoulders, pulling me close so that my side is flush against his. I blink up at him, but his eyes are arrowed in on Toby.

"I believe you are. If I see you sniffing around my woman again, it won't end with an armlock." There's a menace in his quiet voice that might have sent chills down my spine had his arm not been cradling me.

Toby's eyes widen, wariness replacing the bravado. He takes in August's arm around my shoulder. I embrace August and gaze at him adoringly, which doesn't require much acting on my part.

Toby looks at me and the expression that made me finally muster up the courage to break up with him is back in his face. August moves in front of me and takes a step towards Toby. With an angry shout, the younger man finally gets into his car and drives off, tyres screeching.

"Are you okay?" August asks?

"Thank you, Mr. Ford." That's what I call him when he comes to the diner and the odd time I've bumped into him at the orphanage.

August winces, making me wonder what upset him. I've been calling him August in my mind and Mr. Ford when I'm with other people for so long that I'm not at all worried I'll make a mistake in front of him.

"I'll take you home."

The polite thing would be to refuse, to say I don't want to put him out of his way but I'm finally getting a chance to sit close to the man who's haunted my dreams for the last two years so I'm not going to be coy about it.

We make the brief journey to his car in silence. I thank him as he opens the passenger door, then watch his long legs stalk across the front of the car. Not only do I love his deep-set gray eyes, the graying hair at his temples and his enormous size that makes me feel safe, I also find the way he walks sexy. I should think about that icy expression in Toby's eyes just before he left and wonder how I am going to deal with him but being this close to August is making me remember all the times I've spotted his car as I drive home on Fridays and Saturdays nights.

At first, before I realized it was him, I was worried. But when I found out the car belonged to him, for the first time since I began working at Jackson's Diner, I started looking forward to Fridays and Saturdays for another reason other than tips. Then I dared to hope. Hope that he'd fall for me and ask me out.

But six months later, I gave up. August Ford was an experienced man. If he wanted a woman, he didn't have to take such a roundabout way to ask her out. So I came up with another theory. He wanted to make sure I was safe. It wasn't such a far-fetched idea. He grew up at the orphanage, so it was possible he wanted to protect me because I was friends with Mrs. Gallagher (the orphanage director) and an orphan myself.

Whatever the reason, I decided to view him as my guardian angel.

I glance at his muscular hands on the steering wheel, fascinated by the casual way he handles the powerful car. It reminds me of where those skillful hands have been in my dreams, and a curl of desire flickers in my belly. When he looks at me, I turn away, feeling heat creep up my neck and face.

"Why are you walking home alone at this time of night?"

His voice is thick like dark molasses and there's anger in it. I face him. Is he mad he got involved?

"My car broke down. I was going to get a lift with Rosie, but she had an emergency and left early."

"Call a cab next time."

I don't like the commanding tone in his voice, but I remind myself he just saved me from what could have turned into a dangerous situation. Toby was sweet when he was sober. That's why I went out with him in the first place, but when he drank, a mean streak took hold of him.

"I did, but they were giving me an hour's estimated time of arrival and I was too tired to wait that long." I should really have booked a cab as soon as Rosie left, but I was rushed off my feet and didn't have time to do it.

He grunts. He stops at a red light and looks at me. "I'll give you my number. Call me if you can't get a ride after work."

I'm not sure how to respond to that, so I just stare at him.

"If Mrs. Gallagher finds out I knew you were in danger but did nothing to help, she'll pull my ears until they are red. I'm just protecting myself." His lips curve.

I've never seen him smile before. He looks younger, playful even, and that makes him more attractive. I can feel my answering smile.

"I can't imagine Mrs. Gallagher pulling your ears."

"That's because you didn't know her when she was younger. She's softened with age."

The light turns green; he pulls away. "You still haven't given me an answer."

"Okay." I glance around the luxurious car, wishing my house were further away and not a five-minute car ride.

As soon as the vehicle stops, I open the door. August is already being kind to me. I don't want to take up any more of his time.

He gets out of the car and strides round to me.

"I'll walk you to your front door," he says, looking around the low-rise apartment block.

I take the stairs to the second floor, glad that I live in a relatively fine area of Blossom Ford. When I'm in front of my door, I turn to face him. I want to offer him at least a coffee, but am not sure how he'll respond to that.

"I'd like to discuss something with you. Do you have time Sunday?"

It's my only day off. I nod, wondering what is on his mind. "What time?"

We agree on a time and place to meet. Then he watches as I close my front door. I stand with my back against it, listening to his footsteps fade as he walks back down the stairs. Sighing, I throw my bag on the sofa, head to the bathroom, and shower. I can't stop thinking about those hands as he masterfully handled the car and the safe way they made me feel when he embraced me.

As hot water pounds against my skin, my hand glides between my breasts, belly and circles my clit. Pleasure surges as I tip my head back and continue stroking, eyes closed. When I replay August saying I'm his woman in that rough voice of his, I moan and circle faster. I imagine his strong fingers taking over mine, his long middle finger sliding inside me and I come apart with a cry.

Switching off the shower, I shake my head. The nights I sense August following me, I usually stroke myself to sleep. I was too excited to make it to bed tonight.

CHAPTER THREE

August

I WISH I was drinking a double whisky as Ella enters the new coffee shop in town. A burned orange dress hugs her soft brown curves and impossibly high heel sandals cover her feet. I'm not the only one staring. A couple of other men are staring at her, too. She is so beautiful that she turns heads wherever she goes. But I've been near her long enough to know she doesn't even realize the chaos she leaves in her wake.

I stand up and immediately she spots me. A smile that reaches her eyes and makes them crinkle splits her face. And I question what I'm about to do. There's trust in her gaze that no doubt comes from believing Mrs. Gallagher asked me to keep an eye on her. But then I remember Toby's behavior and the doubt slips away.

Once we're both settled with steaming cups of coffee, she looks at me with her large, honey eyes and I know I'll do anything to protect her.

"Have you thought about what you'll do if Toby approaches you again? If I hadn't been there, he would have hit you."

Ella sips her drink, but I don't miss the way her eyes narrow before she looks down at her cup. Having to pack in college after only her first year, burying her parents and taking guardianship of her thirteen-year-old sister all on her own made her independent and self-reliant. She doesn't like it when people try to give her charity. As well as getting involved in her business, I'm being bossy.

I'm trying to be as gentle as I can, but it seems that's something I can't do. It's what Lily, my ex-wife, said when we divorced; that I'm too domineering. But even though I know there's a danger it'll alienate Ella, her safety matters too much for me not to go ahead with my plan.

"You gave him a good scare; I doubt he'll come back."

Something about the way she speaks has my instincts rearing up.

"It's not the first time he's done this since you broke up, is it?"

Ella shrugs. "If he comes back, I'll sort it out."

"How?"

Ella takes another sip of her drink.

"I have a solution that will benefit us both," I say.

She stares at me. "I can handle it."

"Hear me out. We can help each other."

Ella leans forward, searching my face. Her willingness to help others frustrates me yet today it might work in my favor.

"I've been thinking of getting a housekeeper. I'm set in my ways and housekeepers I've had in the past haven't been a good fit because of that. If you're willing to help, the job comes with accommodation - for you and your sister when she's on break from school, holiday pay and flexible hours. Mrs. Gallagher mentioned a while back you wanted to go back to college to finish your degree. This could be a good way of doing it. Especially now Blossom Ford has a college. You don't have to go far. You can study online if you prefer."

I pause. I can almost hear Ella's thoughts; she's interested but suspicious too. I tried to keep the salary low, it's only twice what she's earning now.

I have to up the game, even though what I'm about to tell her is embarrassing to admit. Especially in front of her.

"I live alone. During term time, I'm so busy I don't notice the time passing. But summer breaks, it gets lonely. I'd be glad to have company during dinner, rather than eating alone every day." This is the hardest thing I've had to talk about since my divorce. I'm fucking blushing the way I did when I was fifteen and asked my first crush out on a date.

I gulp my coffee and force myself to peer at Ella.

Compassion is stamped across her face and frustration rears its ugly head again even though I'm happy she's reacted this way.

17

"You're on your own because you want to be. All the single women of Blossom Ford would kill for a date with you. You only need to smile at them."

"What about you?" I can't resist teasing her.

She stares at her coffee. When she finally looks up, there's a huge smile on her face. "I'm just like all the other women. But you're way out of my league." She skims the side of the cup with her index finger.

I'm the one who's out of her league. But I nod. "For this to work well, we should get a marriage of convenience."

Ella chokes on her coffee. I pass her some tissues.

"Sorry," she says when her coughing fit passes. "I was just so surprised."

I wait for her to elaborate.

"You don't have to go that far to help me," she says.

"We're helping each other. We'd have a contract; you can cancel it anytime you want. Marriage carries more weight than a boyfriend/girlfriend relationship. Toby won't bother you if he knows you're married to me and I'll have company in the evenings and a housekeeper who's likely to be more tolerant of me because I'm friends with her friend. When your life changes, you're free to leave. I'm not planning on getting married again, but if things change for me, I'd still need a housekeeper. It's a win-win situation for both of us." The only woman I'd ever want to be married to is Ella, but I keep my voice light.

"Can I think about it? I'd have to leave the diner; I've been there for four years. It's a big decision."

"I only have a few weeks before term starts, it'd be nice to have company before I go back to work. I'm sure the registry office could fit us in with a couple of days' notice." This is better than saying everyday she's living alone there's a chance that dork Toby might harass her.

CHAPTER FOUR

Ella

"YOU MAY KISS THE bride," the Registry Officer says.

My heart pounds harder than a few minutes ago when I said I do. It doesn't seem to matter that this marriage isn't real. Standing in front of August in this white dress is making my heart believe it's real.

There's an expression in his eyes that I can't decipher. He looks into my eyes. His hands reach for the back of my neck. A zing of electricity makes my nerve endings stand to attention. Then his thumbs stroke my cheeks and my breath hitches. I'm frozen, my eyes caught in his, as they slowly snake towards me.

The moment I sense his breath, my eyes close. His lips are soft against mine, a light caress, but they touch the deepest part of me. I've been dreaming of this moment for eons. As if being controlled by a puppet master, I open my lips. He sighs and then his tongue is inside my mouth.

Wanting to be closer to him, I stand on my tiptoes and wrap my arms around his neck. I tilt my head to give him better access.

His tongue inside mine is everything I've dreamed of. In just a few moments August will-

A cough reaches my foggy brain. August lets go of my cheeks and places his arms around my shoulders. I bite my lip as I realize where we are and who's around us. I'm so grateful for August's hands, which stop me from sliding to the floor; my knees are so weak.

Telling myself to get over my still raging hormones and the embarrassment on my cheeks, I nod. August's hands fall away from me. I copy him as he turns towards the Registry Officer. She smiles as she tells us we can go.

A cheering sound booms from behind us and I turn around to see my best friend Winona still whooping and Mrs. Gallagher clapping her hands, her cheeks moist. A piercing arrow of sadness hits my heart and I blink back tears. Would Mom have been crying right now, like Mrs. Gallagher? I shake my head. I've been thinking about Mum and Dad while making my decision, choosing this dress August insisted on paying for, getting ready and walking down the aisle.

When we are outside, Mrs. Gallagher and Winona insist on taking pictures on the vivid greenery of Blossom Ford's Registry office. It's a beautiful day; the sun is shining so strongly, as if to wish us well and make the most of the last few weeks of summer as Winona said, when she was helping me get dressed earlier.

We go to Luigi's for a light meal. It's the classiest restaurant in Blossom Ford. I'd protested against going there, but August said we needed to make sure everyone knew we were married, so there'd be no doubt in Toby's mind about our relationship.

I manage only a few bites and drink a few too many glasses of champagne. When I hug Winona and Mrs. Gallagher goodbye, I can't help shedding a few tears. They are both so hopeful this marriage will work - their optimism touches that deepest recess of my mind wishing for the same thing, even though I should know better.

Mrs. Gallagher knows nothing about the truth of our marriage. I totally agree with August that it'll upset her to know Toby was bothering me. But Winona knows. I had to tell someone, needed someone to sound my ideas on. I should have known that Winona would totally be for this marriage. Since she caught me staring at August one day when he was at the diner last winter, she's known about my crush on him.

I was only glad I'd managed to keep it to myself for a year. Winona had a sixth sense when it came to relationships. She didn't want to admit it, but she was just as good at predicting successful relationships as her mother and female ancestors who run Blossom Ford's ancient, successful matchmaking agency.

"Once you live with him, August will have no hope against your beauty. I've told you a million times that he fancies you. Trust me," she'd said in my apartment the evening August proposed. I'd been too scared to go to her house in case her mother or grandmother heard our conversation.

We are both silent as August drives us home. I can't believe I'm already thinking of his house as home. It's only been four days since he proposed. I bite my lip as my sister Susie pops into my mind. After hours of agonising over what to do, I decided not to tell her I was getting hitched. She's volunteering her medical services in Tanzania during summer break and she's worked so hard to pay for the trip, I didn't have the heart to ask her to come back. Besides, I don't know how things are going to work out with August. It's better not to worry her. She's going straight to Brooklyn when summer break is over. There'll be plenty of time to tell her. I did, however, tell her I rented the apartment and was working as a living in housekeeper for Mr. Ford.

We drive into August's mansion (it's hard to describe it as anything else) and I look around. I'd always wondered what the houses on this side of Blossom Ford looked like inside, after admiring the green lawns outside and large glass windows. I'd always believed it must be bright inside during the summer, with all the sunlight going inside. August's grass is much taller than that of the other houses and his garden isn't as neat, a fact I've overheard many customers at the diner complain about.

When we arrive in front of the front door, he tells me to wait inside. I watch as he moves round to my side and opens the door. A thrill runs through me. I doubt I'll get used to this anytime soon.

I wait for him to walk to the front door so I can follow, but he reaches out and lifts me. I'm so startled, my arms go round him to steady myself.

August laughs. It's a deep sound that goes so well with his voice, but it's innocent too, and my lips tug up.

"We may as well follow tradition, just in case any of my nosy neighbors are watching."

I nod, still shocked at the boyish look on his face. The house stands on its own and the nearest houses are a little farther away, but I know very well one can never be too careful in Blossom Ford.

"My right trouser pocket," August says when we reach the door.

It's a little awkward to get round to his pocket. My hand slides over his muscular thigh and I mumble a sorry before I insert my hand correctly. Triumphantly, I hold the key and look up at him, but he's no longer laughing. Smoldering gray eyes stare down at me, unbridled desire darkening their usual light tone.

My breath catches. But before I can do anything, August's lids slide down and when he looks back up, that burning gaze is gone.

"Can you manage?" he asks lightly.

As I grapple with the door and finally open it, I wonder if I imagined that stare of naked desire.

As soon as we're over the threshold, August puts me down. He shows me around the large kitchen, reception rooms, study, as well as the rooms upstairs. When we reach his room, I stare around the massive bed and furniture. But, apart from a photo of Mrs. Gallagher with her husband and one of August with Mrs. Gallagher in the study, there aren't any other pictures. My heart wrenches. This is a beautiful house. Why does it look like there's not much life inside it?

CHAPTER FIVE

August and Ella

AS I PULL OUT the few pans in the kitchen drawers, flashes of the wedding night of my first marriage go through my mind. I wince at the hope I had then. I believed Lily and I were so in love we'd grow old together. I wanted to spend all my free time with her and showered her with what I thought was affection. Lily called it being clingy. I will not make the mistakes I made with her again. I'm going to give Ella space, even if all I want to do is spend as much time with her as possible. Footsteps sound by the door and I turn towards them.

Ella's wearing a baby blue track suit and fluffy black slippers. I've never seen her looking so cute and soft. Warmth spreads through me. I want to see her every day like this. I'm not sure if it's because she's not wearing make-up or the fact we're in our indoor clothes, but there's a sense of intimacy in the kitchen.

"Sorry I'm late; I dozed off."

There's a tentative air about her, like she's not sure how she'll be welcomed. As if she's decided, she tucks her sleek, shoulder-length, black hair behind her ears and comes to examine the pots.

"Is this all you've got?" she asks.

I smile, hoping it'll relax her.

"I can use these two. Do you have pasta?"

I nod and head towards a cupboard. She goes to the fridge, rummages there and returns with lettuce and tomatoes.

"Pasta and tomato sauce with salad it is. I'll go grocery shopping tomorrow."

"We'll go together. Remember the companionship side of our agreement? Also, it'll be beneficial to be seen around town."

Ella's eyes are enormous, but she nods.

"My cooking repertoire consists of grilled cheese and peanut butter sandwiches. So, tell me what to do."

Ella laughs and shakes her head. More warmth spreads through me. I stand beside her as we prepare the food, my part mostly cutting ingredients. I've seen her laugh at the diner and orphanage, but knowing she's laughing because of me has me wrapped up in knots.

"How did you learn to cook?" I ask as she stirs onions in olive oil, totally absorbed in what she's doing.

After a couple of heartbeats, she looks up. "My mom taught me. She'd wait until Dad got home and washed up, then she'd order us to cut and wash vegetables and bring anything she needed. Susie and I were also the tasters." There's a smile in her voice, but I can also hear sadness.

"Would you rather not talk about them?"

Ella shakes her head and her jet-black hair sways on her shoulders. "Talking about them helps to keep their memory alive." She stops and grins.

"What is it?"

"Flour."

"What?" I ask, a little confused but enthralled by the mischievous look that transforms her expression.

"Dad once spilled a bag of flour while opening it. It went all over his clothes. I must have been about eight at the time and the sight of his immense body, hair and beard covered in fluffy white flour was too much for me. I burst out laughing. Dad tried to take revenge, and a war broke out. After that, Mom insisted we wore our oldest clothes whenever we were making pastry."

"Sounds like you had fun cooking with your family." I would love to have that with her; to cook and play with Ella and our kids.

"Put the carrots in," Ella watches as I carefully slide the grated orange bits into the pan. She holds out the spoon.

I grab it and stir.

"There's a rota for chores at the orphanage. I would have thought you'd be a decent cook."

"Cook and I didn't get along. Since kitchen duty was the only chore that ended with a treat, I always avoided her by swapping with one of the other kids." When I was little, I didn't understand why Cook treated me differently from the other kids. It only made sense after I started school and learned why the other kids called me a sign of bad luck. "I guess you can teach me," I change the subject.

There's compassion in Ella's eyes. Some of the old folks in town still walk the other way when they see me so she probably knows my story. She looks like she's going to say more, but then she turns to the stove and says, "Add a little water."

She stands there looking at me, making me feel like a pupil. "What were you studying in college?" I ask because the notion of Ella watching me is turning me on.

"Finance." She checks the pasta and grabs a kitchen towel. "I didn't know what I wanted to do, but I was good with numbers, so I chose that. It's only now I've volunteered at the orphanage that I've learned running a place like that is what I'd like to do."

"Mrs. Gallagher would hire you straight away."

"Did you always want to be a professor?" Ella asks.

"No. I love studying living organisms, so I was a researcher for years before one of my professors asked me to cover him for a few months. I loved it and now I do both."

As we cook and eat, we talk about my work and Ella's family's amusing kitchen antics. The sun is setting by the time we finish. When Ella asks if I'd like to sit outside and watch the golden rays descend on the horizon, I lead the way, taking the bottle of wine we started drinking.

We sit mostly in silence. After our time in the kitchen, the quiet is comfortable, as if two good friends are sitting side by side. I realize the last time I watched the sun set was the day I graduated high school and left Blossom Ford. Before that, I used to sneak out of the orphanage to watch the sunset at Blossom Ford Point.

Weekends, the place was busy with groups of young people hanging out, but during most weekdays, there was only the murmur of the river - and in the spring the cherry blossom petals falling on the ford - to keep me company. The solitude was bliss after the chaos of the orphanage.

"It's late. I should go to bed." There's a reluctance in Ella's voice that's egging me to ask her to stay longer. I tamp down on the urge, reminding myself she's here so I can keep her safe.

"Goodnight." My voice betrays nothing of the need to hold her, kiss those strawberry lips and have Ella's body flush against mine.

Ella

AUGUST AND I are visiting the orphanage. I volunteer a couple of days a month, helping with cooking, mending clothes and linen, but I didn't know August also volunteered. So far, he's taken care of odd jobs inside the main building as well as mowed the lawn.

I have never been this kind of happy before. Cooking and eating all my meals with August and sitting in the garden in the evenings with him, drinking wine and talking brings me a contentment I never thought I'd have with him.

I've also never been this kind of frustrated before. The day of the wedding, I know I didn't mistake the red-hot embers in August's eyes when we kissed at the church and before he carried me into the house. Even if I had, almost every day I catch him looking at me, the desire in his eyes so raw, I know he wants me as much as I want him.

But he does nothing about it. Toby was my first boyfriend and since we only lasted four months, I have little experience with men, but I've tried everything I know to seduce him short of walking out naked in front of him. Shorts that are almost indecent and off the shoulder tops darken his gaze and make him steal more glances of me, but they don't make him touch me.

For the last two weeks, I've been alternating between bliss and frustration. And it's getting harder not to show. Something else bothers me. I've shared so much with August but I can't help feeling he's keeping a distance from me. Sure, I'm normally a chatty person, but I don't share my personal life with everyone. August makes me want to share. And I like the way talking about my family and dreams seems to make him happy. I like that he's smiling more and more.

I'm carrying a basket of linen when I spot August in the small room Mrs. Gallagher keeps for any of the kids that want a quiet place to study. He's tutoring a sixteen-year-old who's graduating from high school next year. I shake my head at the hero worship going on. Just like August, Leo wants to be a biologist.

August is saying something I can't hear, but his expression has me catching my breath. He's engrossed. His total focus is on making sure Leo understands whatever he's tutoring. My heart skips a beat and in that moment, I realize I've fallen in love with August Ford. I'm helplessly in love with the way he looks at me like I'm the only woman in the world.

As if he's aware someone is watching him, he looks towards me. I bolt. I can't pretend I'm not affected by him. The laundry room is empty, I take refuge in it.

When I was young, I'd always fantasized about falling in love. It was going to be a wonderful moment. However, worry fills me as I pick up a sheet, find a tear and begin mending. August's guardedness and refusal to touch me makes me worry that although he might fancy me, deep down he really views me as a very young friend of someone he loves rather than the woman I want him to see me as. It's alright for him to help me, but I'm starting to feel like he doesn't believe I can cope with the deepest worries of his life.

CHAPTER SIX

August

AS SOON AS I wake up, a wave of sorrow and desolation pull me into the deepest abyss and I remember what day it is. August the thirty-first. This day has come round too quickly. Usually, a couple of days before, I'll know it's coming. For the first time since I realized Mrs. Gallagher's husband, Kenzie Gallagher, died on this day trying to save me and my mother, who jumped into the river, I didn't go through the usual warning period.

It's because of Ella. Every day we've spent together, I've fallen more and more for her. I was in love with her before. Now it's like I can't function properly without her. I can tell by the darkness outside that it's not dawn yet. From experience, I know there's no point in going back to bed. I strip and don on my running sweats.

I tiptoe out of the house. Outside, I inhale the heaviness of a day getting ready for rain. I head towards Blossom Ford Point. As I get there, the first rays of sunshine are coming through the horizon. I sit underneath the cherry blossom tree, right in front of the ford, and watch the water gurgle down the river.

I love and hate this place. The peace here settles my mind a little. I pick up a soft, pink petal and stroke it. It reminds me of Ella's smile. I smile at how badly I have the hots for her.

I shake my head to rid myself of the sense of guilt I feel towards Kenzie Gallagher and stare around me at the luscious greenery along the river and mountain in the distance. Mrs. Gallagher said although no one knew my mother as she was new in town, she must have wanted me to have a beautiful after life, that's probably why she chose this wonderful river as a resting place for us. But I often wondered how anyone could bear to hurt a child in such a beautiful place.

Mrs. Gallagher has only ever given me love, still, every time I see her, I wonder how different her life would be if her husband were still alive.

After a couple of hours, when the sun is hotter on my face, I get up and head home. I'm not good company, but Ella will wonder where I am. I arrive as she's getting out of her room.

"I didn't hear you go out," she says, her face a study in curiosity.

"I went out for a jog."

I shower and dress, then join her in the kitchen. I make short work of my pancakes and eggs.

"Now that term's about to start, I have a lot of work to catch up on," I say and head to the study, leaving her to wash up alone.

I've tried to be my usual self, but I can tell she knows something is up by the curious looks she gave me over breakfast.

I spend most of the day in the study, keeping myself busy. When Ella comes in to tell me it's lunchtime, she's looking so lovely in shorts and an off the shoulder top, that I'm not sure I can trust my ironclad self-control in the mood I'm in so I ask her for sandwiches. She nods but her smile falters. I frown at her back as she leaves the room. It's the first time we're not eating together, so I thought she might actually like to have some alone time.

When she brings in a tray, her usual friendly expression is back and I'm relieved. By late afternoon, I know I need to take a break when words start blurring in front of me. I move to the small couch in the room and lie down to rest.

When I come to myself, something soft is touching my lips in the lightest of caresses. The scent of strawberries reaches my nostrils and I inhale, my eyes flying open because I recognize the sweet fragrance and can no longer feel that soft caress.

Honey eyes stare at me with a longing as deep and strong as my own. Ella's face is only a couple of inches from mine. My arm snakes out and pulls it towards mine until our lips are touching again. The movement is so natural, as if this is what I was meant to do.

Soft sighing is a beautiful song in the room, but I don't know if it's coming from me or Ella. Her lips taste as wonderful as they did at the church. No, better.

I move my lips from side to side against hers, the ensuing sensation shooting electricity straight to my cock and just like that, I'm hard and my body demands more.

I angle my head and with my tongue tease the seam of her red lips. Immediately they part and this time, I can tell the sigh is coming from Ella.

She lets me in and caresses my cheeks. Her touch is so strong, so sure and her response so assuredly hot, that even as my tongue duels with hers, one of my hands moves towards her body.

She shifts closer until her top half is lying flush against mine. Her hands move to my head and she strokes my curls.

I trail my fingers across her chest until I find one breast. She arches as if to give me more access when I kneed it softly. I caress the nipple through the thin top and Ella moans. The sound is so sweet I want to hear more of it. I let go of the back of her neck and touch her other breast too, so that I'm caressing both of her nipples. My lips curve as her moans increase.

I've dreamed of caressing Ella's generous breasts for so long. It's better than my imagination.

"Does it feel good?" I ask as I pinch a hard point.

Ella arches her back further and says something.

"What do you want? Tell me!" I can't believe how sandy my voice is. It brooks no argument, but right now my mind is filled with desire and pleasing Ella, I can't make myself speak in a gentler tone.

"Shirt off!" Ella's voice is raspy too. She arches towards me and I help her slide the offending garment off. The lacy blue bra framing her cups is so beautiful that I want to touch it, but Ella's unclipped the bra so I help her with that too. She's so beautiful. I reach up and pull her on top of me.

Then we're kissing again. I've wanted to touch her so badly I snake my hand past her chest and the lush brown skin of her belly until my hands come across the button of her shorts. She lifts a bit and I undo it. I slip my hands inside her panties and curve them around her ass, kneading the soft skin.

She glides against my cock, and it rears up towards her.

I focus on her. This is my fantasy - pleasuring her. My hands massage round her voluptuous ass and hips until I'm playing with the patch of hair on her mound. I inch my hand until it finds her clit. I give it a couple of strokes. Slowly, I rub it from side to side. Ella moans then buries her mouth against my neck, sucking the skin there.

I groan. Touching her feels so good, but the added sensation at my throat almost unmans me. I'm so sensitive there. Inhaling deeply, I focus on what I was doing. I want to see Ella come apart in my arms. So I concentrate on the soft noises she's making, use them to guide me.

I slip my middle finger into her wet pussy, even as I rub the heel of my hand against her hard nub.

"August..." her raw murmur is a breath and a demand.

I insert another digit and scissor both fingers then twist, increasing the pace until she's writhing uncontrollably against my hand.

She arches and I pinch her nipple. Ella comes apart, my name a beautiful song around us.

Smiling, I stroke her back as she lies on my chest, as limp as a rag doll.

Yet moments later, her hand slides between us, and when it touches my cock, my smile vanishes.

"I want to give you pleasure too. And I want your skin on mine." She's a little shy, but the truth in her voice is clear. It spreads a warmth in my heart and turns my already hard shaft into steel.

"Aww Ella, let me take my shirt off."

She lets go of me. I slide out from underneath her and she turns until she's lying on her back.

I rip my shirt off and throw it aside. Something catches the corner of my eye and I look up into my reflection on the mirror on the opposite side of my desk. Reality comes knocking in.

I take a couple of breaths to steady myself. To bring back my rigid self-control.

"August." Ella's arm reaches up to me.

I swallow. I want to take her hand, lie back down and fuck her until she's so sated, she can't speak.

I shake my head and turn away. I can't do this to Ella. Instead of ravishing her, I should protect her. Even if it's from me. I clear my throat.

"I'm so sorry Ella. That shouldn't have happened. It isn't fair to you."

Then I grab my shirt and march out of there as if the hounds of hell are chasing me. Because staying means taking her soft body and I love Ella too much to let her be involved with a man who's broken and too old for her. The beautiful, strong young woman that she is deserves better.

CHAPTER SEVEN

Ella

IT'S THE LAST WEEK of September and I can tell fall is coming. There's a nip in the air during the days and it's much colder in the evenings. I wrap my hands more tightly around the mug of cocoa I've been nursing and, for what feels like the millionth time, try to make myself focus on the notes I took during my first year of college.

It doesn't work. I've been spacing out so much I'm starting to worry about myself. I poke the curtain aside and peer into the darkness outside. The front drive is as quiet as a morgue. August's going to be late again.

Since that day, I've only seen him twice. Even then, I think it was by accident. He's like a spy, who comes in the dead of night, leaves at the crack of dawn and moves silently around the house.

"I'm sorry Ella. You're here under my protection. I shouldn't have done that to you," he'd said both times I tried to talk to him.

I wanted to scream that he'd given me the best orgasm of my life. But he'd vanished as soon as he said the words.

Meals don't taste the same as they did when I ate with him. The house seems massive and unwelcome, even though I put up pictures of August and me with Mrs. Gallagher and the kids the day we visited the orphanage. The flowers I place in the kitchen and sitting room don't brighten the house as much as they used to.

It's late. After giving up on my notes, I get ready for bed. I lie awake under the covers until I hear August. I rush to the door as silently as I can and inch it open just in time to see his bedroom door close.

I return to bed. When I wake up the next morning, he's gone.

Now that August is working and not eating at home, I spend more time at the orphanage. More and more, I love my time there. I've started helping with the books as well, using the skills I learned my first year at college.

I'm taking a break in the garden, sitting on an old wooden bench when Mrs. Gallagher comes out and throws herself beside me, her short bob of white hair a little messed up. It's been a busy morning even though I loved every minute. Not having a moment to think about the pain in my heart is a blessing.

We watch a frog leap in the pond a few steps away from us.

"Something has been bothering you," Mrs. Gallagher says.

I smile. Despite her gnarled hands and rickety legs, Mrs. Gallagher's eyes are still as sharp as my mother's. I could hide nothing from her, either. Talking to a friend helps me most times, but I can't talk to my sister about this and Winona's been so busy with her postgraduate studies, I've been mulling over things by myself.

There isn't anyone in Blossom Ford that knows August the way Mrs. Gallagher does, however I don't know how to broach the subject. It's like talking to a mother-in-law about marital problems. Besides, she doesn't know our marriage is a contract.

"Is August not treating you well? It's very clear he's in love with you, but he can be a moody man."

"He's very kind."

Mrs. Gallagher snorts. "Something's wrong." She stares at me, as if she can pull out the answer from my mind.

"I think my age makes him feel overprotective, so he doesn't share a lot with me." I shrug.

Mrs. Gallagher plays with the plain band around her ring finger. "That's how my Kenzie was at the beginning of our marriage." She suddenly cracks up in laughter.

I stare at her. "How did you deal with it?"

"I was only eighteen when I came to Blossom Ford as a mail-order bride. There were nearly twenty years between us, but one look was all it took me to fall in love. From that moment on, Kenzie had no chance. I took the lead."

I laugh with Mrs. Gallagher, some of the stiffness in my heart easing.

I take a couple of days to decide what to do. I know I can't go on like this. August's beautiful house is meant to be shared, but I'm no longer comfortable here. I want him to see me as a woman who loves him. Someone who wants to share his burdens the way he's shared mine. Even if all I can do for him is listen.

There's no doubt he's attracted to me and enjoys my company. It's time for him to decide if what he feels for me is strong enough to overcome whatever's been keeping him away from me.

When he sneaks into his room at one in the morning, I'm waiting for him in the love seat under the window.

He switches the light and drops his bag by the door. His tie comes off next. He looks as sexy as sin, but even from here, I notice the shadows under his eyes. His beard is a little wild, as if he hasn't trimmed it in a while. My fingers itch to touch the smattering of gray hairs there. I need to be in control of my emotions, so I shut down those thoughts just as August notices me.

"What are you doing here?" His voice is curt with surprise and something else – longing. It's there in the way his eyes rove over me before he turns his back and opens the door. "Go to bed."

Before, if he'd spoken to me like that, I would leave, but not today.

"We either talk here or I come to campus. Choose."

He scowls at me, but I stay seated.

A sigh and I know that for now, he's going to listen. He leaves the door wide open and leans on the wall, arms crossed.

"I can't carry on staying here, the way things are between us."

August raises one brow. I stow my hands under me to hide the fear surging at his lack of a better response.

"We're keeping to our bargain quite well." Impartiality coats every cord of his voice.

"I'm not happy, and neither are you. I've driven you away from your home."

"I'm working- "

"That's bullshit!"

August inhales. His arms are steel bars around his body.

I stand up, unable to sit. I walk closer to him. His eyes slide to the open doorway and hurt tightens my chest.

"Do you hate spending time with me that much?" I blink but can't help the tears in my voice.

Anguish spreads across his face. "You're the best thing in my life."

"Then why drive me away?"

"How can I not?" He shoves his hand through his hair. "I want the best for you."

"That's you."

"The harbinger of death? A man who's too old for you and has so many scars he's terrified of even losing your friendship? Me loving you will forever remain a dream of mine."

Sorrow for August threatens to weaken me, but his last words speed up my heartbeat.

As if realizing what he just admitted, he marches to the door and stands there, face away from me.

I close the distance between us, but I don't leave. I'm never leaving. Not after he's admitted he loves me. I plant my feet shoulder length apart, wrap my arms around his back and lean my head on his broad chest. He's as tense as a coiled panther.

"I love you too." I inject every ounce of truth in those four words. Three times, I repeat that tiny sentence. When nothing changes, I say, "I'm a woman who's mothered a stroppy teenager and can take care of herself. I don't want a younger man. All your scars make you August Ford. I'm in love with August Ford."

A choked sound rumbles from his chest. But he doesn't budge.

Neither do I. "Before you single-handed decided not to love me, I was having the happiest time of my life with you. Instead of making us miserable, you can choose to make both of us happy."

I don't know how long we stand like that before his arms inch around me. He stays like that and I think he's breathing in the scent on my hair because his head is resting lightly on mine and I can hear his chest rising rhythmically.

My feet are getting uncomfortable when he lifts me up and carries me to the bed. He lays me down gently, gets in beside me and pulls me toward him, my head on his chest.

I lose consciousness. Muted rays of sunshine cast shadows in the room when I wake up. I'm still lying on August's chest. Carefully, I turn my head. He's staring at me.

Heat creeps up my neck. "Have you been watching me sleep?"

"Yes."

I put my head back where it was before I woke up, away from his probing eyes.

His chest rumbles under my cheek.

"Where's the strong woman who successfully dealt with a stroppy teenager?"

"Give me a few minutes," I quip back from my safe position, happy he's teasing me.

He turns my head towards him.

"I love you," August says quietly, looking straight into my eyes. "I'm not always the easiest of people to live with. I might try and sort things out on my own or share more than you can handle, but I'll always love you."

I think about what he's just said. Knowing that he loves me has given me superhuman strength, where he's concerned.

"The more you share with me, the closer I'll be to you. It's when you don't share that it hurts me. I'm the staying kind of person. But if you're being a pain in the ass, I'll tell you." My voice is as quiet as his.

He searches my gaze until he seems to find whatever he's looking for. Ever so gently, he kisses my forehead.

My heart melts. I want him to feel this amazing sensation too, so I slide up his body to kiss his wide forehead too. My thigh touches something hard. August groans, his face twisted into what seems to me like pleasure and pain.

I stop, totally distracted. I reach my hand toward his cock and gently squeeze it. Another groan is strangled out of August.

I smile and move downwards. I unbuckle his belt, remove it, and toss it aside. An urge to see him grows. I undo the button on his pants and reach inside his black briefs. His cock jerks in my hand. I pull it out, careful not to hurt him.

August's hands tighten against my shoulders.

"That feels so good, honey."

A compliment has never sounded so sweet. I lick my lips. My pussy clenches. I stroke my hand up and down his long, wide length. A spurt across the top catches my attention. Using my free hand, I flick a long fingernail across the slit there, pushing the viscous liquid into the hand sliding up and down, making the glide smoother.

"Yes, just like that." His hips lift towards my hands.

I want to sing. To have driven August to this helpless state feels amazing. But after a couple more pumps, he stops me.

"I can't last long."

August shakes his head, even as he is pulling me up. He sits beside me and starts unbuttoning his shirt. "I want to be inside you."

I remove my clothes too.

"You're the most beautiful woman I've ever seen, Ella." Need darkens August's eyes as they snake across my body.

Before I can answer him, he's kissing me. We fall onto the wide bed, our limbs tangling.

"I'm ready."

August slides a finger into my slippery folds. I'm so wet, more of my juices run down my thigh.

"Take me now," I say as hard as I can before August nips one on my nipples and I can only moan.

"Say that again."

He nips my other nipple.

"Make me yours," I say after my moan has died.

He pushes into me a little and pauses. I suck in a breath as I feel myself stretching around him.

"Okay?" A stroke down my cheek.

I nod and push up.

He keeps inching and stopping until he's all the way in. I bite his neck. Just like I hoped, he groans and pumps involuntarily into me.

"Tease," he says, the sweat beads on his forehead making him sexier.

When he finally starts moving, his strokes are so powerful, like he can't control himself anymore. I wrap my legs around his ass and meet every single thrust, the tension inside me coiling until I unravel, his name a voiceless sob.

After only a few more thrusts, August groans as he spurts into me, causing me to shudder with more contractions.

"You're mine, Ella Ford."

"And you're mine, August Ford."

EPILOGUE

August

Four Years Later

I HUNG UP THE phone and shake my head at Ella.

"He's not coming?" She asks loudly amid chattering, music and excited kids' screams in our neatly manicured garden.

"The way his voice sounded; I doubt he'll be leaving his house anytime soon."

"You feel sorry for Caleb, don't you? Now he's in town you are hoping you can help him start socializing again."

"I know what it's like to be distant and different from everyone around you. For a powerful man to be suddenly confined to a wheelchair is hell. It's a shame because in college he lit up any party. He's a good friend. I don't want him to shut himself off and suffer alone."

"Not being able to walk when it used to be as easy as breathing must be hard," Ella says.

"Daddy, I need you," Sophie's chubby hands pull at my leg as strongly as a determined three-year-old can.

Ella laughs. "Careful, you'll drop Daddy."

Sophie scoffs as if Ella's words are silly, her chocolate eyes rolling theatrically. "Mommy, don't you know how strong Daddy is?"

"You're right Poppet. Daddy is superman."

Ella shakes her head, still laughing. I pass Kenzie to her and watch as our little boy wraps his tiny arms around Ella. I can't believe how good I've become at holding a baby with one hand while doing something else with the other.

I pick up Sophie, hoist her onto my shoulders. "Lead the way," I say.

She points towards the party hostess and I head to the back of the garden where my sister-in-law and a small group of pre-schoolers are running around. My chest is filled with pride and happiness as I pass a few of my colleagues, Mrs. Gallagher, a couple of people from town and two women from Ella's part-time college course.

I turn back, my eyes seeking her out. She's passing Kenzie to Mrs. Gallagher. I smile, even though Ella is not looking at me. Her love, trust and acceptance have helped me to realize that I'm someone that deserves a happy life.

"Daddy, hurry!" The impatience in my little girl's voice reminds me so much of my wife, that I can't help laughing as I do as I am told.

MARRYING THE BROKEN BOSS

CURVY BRIDES OF BLOSSOM FORD BOOK 2

IRIS WEST

CHAPTER ONE

Tiana

I RUN AS SOON as the bus door opens. I hate being late. My number one rule is Do Not Be Late. Even though I know better, I ask myself why the bus had to be late today of all days when I usually can tell the time by Blossom Ford busses.

A car is coming in the opposite direction, but I figure I have enough time to cross the street. I sprint, avoiding a big puddle of water on the side of the road, but a couple of steps onto the pavement, a cold rush stops me. I glance at my front and side. They are both wet and so is part of my face and hair.

I turn around, but the car is already roaring off in the distance. A string of curses comes out of me before I can stop it. Now I'm late and messy. Even the image of Mum standing with her hands on her hips, saying she's gonna wash my mouth with soap, doesn't stop the cuss words. I set off again and sigh when I spot the humongous old house with a wrap-around porch.

I push the bell at the large gate, the butterflies that started dancing earlier this morning doing acrobatics with the added worry of my lateness and visual. I don't want my patient to think I'm a rag doll when we meet for the first time. Not patient, I correct myself, client. And a filthy rich one at that. If he takes me on as his physical therapist, he'll be my boss for the foreseeable future.

"Yes?" The voice is terse over the intercom.

"It's Tiana Remington, the physical therapist."

The intercom buzzes, and the gate swings open when I push it. I race up the long drive, fisting my free hand. I worked hard during my training period and the following years at a rehab centre to know I'm very good at what I do. But this is only my second private gig, and the agency warned me to make sure I'm extra professional with Mr. cooper. There's nothing I can do about the tardiness but I have to do something about my appearance.

Near the front door, I whisk out a mirror and peer at my face and head. I get tissues from my bag and dab wet skin and hair, glad my eye liner only ran a little. There's no time to retouch my make-up. The tissue is only leaving white bits on my clothes, so I give up. I say a prayer of thanks that my top is dark blue and my trousers are even darker, then tell myself to stow away my mirror.

"Is checking your make-up when you're late part of the pro-fessionalism you mentioned in your resume?"

I gulp, feeling like a kid caught red-handedly shoving a hand into the cookie jar. I stare in the voice's direction and my breath catches. It's been a long time since I've seen such an amazing posture. A chest that makes me think the man at the door must work out daily, offsets a straight back and square shoulders, even though he's in a wheelchair. He has green eyes, dark brown hair and a beard I want to pet. I realize I'm staring and clear my throat.

"Mr. Cooper?" Where's my usually calm voice?

"Let's get started, shall we?"

Breathe, I tell myself. I am a professional. I'm good at my job. Being turned on by a man's great posture doesn't make me weird. It's normal, cause I'm human. Also, I will not crush on my boss, I recite as I rush after him. I get in the house just in time to see Mr. Cooper enter a room off the hallway.

I close the door and march to the room. As I walk in, he doesn't take his eyes off me. Shaping my lips into my most professional smile, which makes the grumpiest of patients smile back, I hold out my hand.

"We've lost enough time. Let's begin."

I just about keep the smile in place and sit in the chair facing him, putting my bag on the floor. He's mad, I get it. I'd be mad too if I'd been as late as I am, but his rudeness is disconcerting.

"If you can't get here on time, why should I have you as my physical therapist?"

I purse my lips to stop the explanation of how I'd actually left extra early to ensure I got here ahead of time, but the bus had broken down and the next one had been late too. There was an air about Caleb Cooper that screamed of confidence, strength and self-discipline. He wouldn't care about excuses.

I look at him and make my voice strong. "I want to open a private practice by the time I'm 30. Being financially stable is crucial to me. As you will have heard from the client that recommended me, I know what I'm doing. I'm very discreet and am willing and able to carry out any other housekeeping or administrative tasks you may require. I believe those are the requisites you're looking for. There was an unavoidable circumstance today. I apologize; it won't happen again." Heartbreak over Mum and Dad's rows about money before their bitter divorce taught me the importance of money.

He searches my face for a while, then nods and interlaces his fingers over his knees.

Inside, I do a little dance of gratitude as I take out my tablet and find the files his doctor and previous physical therapist sent. I studied them last night, so I just need to ask a few questions and take down any new information before we come up with a treatment plan that'll work for him.

"What do you think is the biggest challenge to your mobility now?" I ask and discover it's not just his posture I like. He answers my questions and asks his own with knowledge that shows he's done a great deal of research about his spinal cord injury.

CHAPTER TWO

Caleb

ARROWS OF PAIN SHOOT through my lower body as I take a step, then another, but I ignore them and force myself to carry on.

"That's it Caleb, you're nearly there. Keep going."

There's such a beautiful tilt to Tiana's voice. That, combined with the way she encourages me to keep going, makes me feel like there are only the two of us in the world. I want to please her, and that gives my tired body a boost.

She's walking beside me, repeating those silly words of encouragement.

"Five more steps. I'm counting with you. One, two..."

I make the last step, gripping the bars I installed in this room to help finish my rehabilitation.

"Well done! I've got you now. Put your arm on my shoulder."

I hesitate.

"Okay?"

I lift one hand off the bar and hers immediately grabs it. She puts the hand across the back of her neck and wraps her free arm around me. Tiana's tall and curvy, but her body is no match for my enormous frame of six feet-three inches, so I carry as much of my weight as I can.

She's saying something about how strong my posture is; I let her words warm me as I sit in my wheelchair.

"I'll grab a bottle of cold water," she says.

I'm exhausted, but my eyes still watch her curvy butt sway in those black yoga pants she wears. Tiana and I have worked together for five days now, and my attraction to her has only grown stronger. I've been meaning to apologize to her for the rude way I behaved when we met, but I don't know how to.

I doubt, sorry I was so attracted by the sight of you when no woman has made me the least bit interested in the last six months that I was a jerk, would work. Not when she arrives a good fifteen minutes before the start of every shift, gives her all during therapy sessions and is efficient at organizing my mail and carrying out tasks.

She's an excellent cook, too. Her meals are nutritious and meet the demands specified in her treatment plan. I've seen that drive in young men and women who became successful entrepreneurs. Once again, I wonder why money is so important to her.

Nevertheless, I have to apologize. I still can't believe I was embarrassed and took it out on a twenty-five-year-old woman.

I'm nearly twenty years older than her! Before I met Tiana, the only other woman I've ever been embarrassed around is Granny.

I'm an expert on pleasing women; there is not a single woman I was ever interested in I wasn't able to charm. It looks like I lost my touch along with my mobility when I had the car accident. My lips tug up. It's no wonder I'm smiling at myself. A lot of my lovers would love to throw that bit of information at me if they found out.

Tiana strides back into the room. She hands me a water bottle and turns.

"You're welcome to stay," I say, thinking of making amends. "You can have your breaks here if you don't mind spending your free time with the boss."

A smile splits her face, stretching her almond-shaped eyes even more. "I'll get my water."

She's back a few moments later. "You're very good at your job. Sorry about the way I behaved when you turned up," I say after she sits down, cross-legged on the floor.

Chestnut colored eyes stare at me before she smiles again. I realize then that I like her eyes.

"I hate it when others are late too," Tiana confesses. "This is a lovely house. I'm glad it's finally occupied and I get to be inside it. I've loved looking at it since I was little."

"My mother used to love it, too. She chose all the current furnishings and paints. When I leave for Garnet City, I'll have to think of what to do with it."

"You're not thinking of selling it, are you? It'd be a shame to lose a place like this."

There's genuine alarm in her face; it makes me curious about her. "Not soon." I love this place because I was happy here as a kid, but being here without my parents is a little hard.

"How did you know you wanted to become a physical therapist?" From a young age, I learned everything I needed to help Granny manage our family company. Luckily for me, I loved every minute.

"When I was in junior school, we went on a school trip to the home for the elderly. A couple of physical therapists were working with some residents and I thought it was so cool, the way they could help others walk. From that day, I didn't think of being anything else."

I wish Tiana being late was the only reason I was angry at her. I tell myself I'm so attracted to her because I've abstained from sex for too long. My body is getting fitter; it's perfectly natural to be attracted to a stunningly beautiful woman. There's nothing wrong with liking her. I've liked many of my lovers in the past.

What's worrying me is that I'm thinking of Tiana when I wake up in the mornings. When she leaves the house in the evenings, I smile at the way she said something during therapy. I look forward to her arriving for work. The sense that she brings sunshine into the dark world of pain and fear of never walking again I descended into after the accident, is increasing. That's not me. I don't do this type of liking a woman.

Her massages are supposed to relax my legs, yet her firm hands make me think about what else she can do with them. I can accept that. It's pure pleasure, something I excel in. And if Tiana weren't so young or a small-town girl that might just be looking for a relationship, a lot more would have happened between us than charged looks. Because I know women enough to tell she's attracted to me.

However, I don't do relationships. They lead to things like love. And love leads to loss so profound that makes a ten-year-old boy stop talking. The way it did when Mum and Dad died in a car accident. I never want to experience that type of pain again. Once was enough.

My phone vibrates. I pull it out of my trouser pocket and chek the name on the screen. It's Daniel, my second in command. Only he's so well-groomed at the business, he never rings unless something is massively wrong.

"Your granny's collapsed, she's in hospital right now," he says once I answer.

Dread fists my heart. "Where?"

"Garnet City General. I'll organize the plane."

"Send me any details you have over the phone." I hung up, mind racing.

"Is everything okay?" Tiana asks.

"I have to fly to Garnet City. I'll call as soon as I figure out what's happening."

CHAPTER THREE

Caleb

DRIVING THROUGH RUSH HOUR traffic in Garnet City makes me realize how much I love the quieter streets of Blossom Ford. It's like I've left one state to go to another when both places are in Arizona. As the car approaches the hospital, I put my mask on, in case I run into reporters. But getting out of the car, into the hospital and going up the elevator to the private room Granny's in, is uneventful.

"I'm very sorry to tell you it's stage four cancer," the doctor says when I see him.

I hoped it was something like a heavy cold; this throws me. Granny's lived a long, fulfilling life, but she's the only family I have. I'm terrified of losing her.

"How are you going to treat her?"

The doctor pushes his glasses up his nose and I know it's going to be bad.

"She's ninety-three, so operating is out of the question. Chemotherapy is going to be our best bet."

"Can you cure her?" I'm a kid clutching at straws.

"If Mrs. Cooper responds well to treatment, we can prolong her life."

By the time I finish talking to the doctor, I just want to see Granny and hug her. She is asleep when I wheel my chair into her room, after thanking the nurse who held the door open for me.

Granny looks so tiny the bed doesn't seem to have anyone in it. As I get closer, her white curls shine and I can see her face. It's smaller than the last time I saw her, which was only three days ago. When I came to live with her at the age of ten, she was huge to my younger self. Over the years, she raised and groomed me to take over the family's beauty business and only stepped down from management fifteen years ago.

"Caleb." Hearing her voice when she wakes up makes me feel a little better.

I hug her, careful not to hurt her.

"Help me sit up," she says.

"You just had to up one on me, didn't you, Mrs. Cooper?" I say after she's sitting up with her glasses on. I deliberately use the nickname I gave her when I was in high school.

"The only way to beat me is to get out of that wheelchair. How are your legs doing?"

"I'm walking short distances."

"That's really good." She caresses the blanket, taking an interest in the patterns there.

I know Granny. She has something on her mind. When she looks up at me again, the steadiness in her green eyes so like mine and the way she's holding her chin, tell me she's decided on something.

"I don't know how much longer I have. I want to see you settled."

I swallow. "What about all the kids I gave you?"

She laughs. "I bet you're the only grandson in the world who opens a children's centre when his granny asks for grandchildren."

"You love spending time with the kids. You're there nearly every day, it was a waste of money hiring a manager."

"I'm there to play with the kids, not manage the place."

"I'll pretend I believe that."

"Now, don't get me off topic." All amusement leaves her face, and she becomes serious again. "I don't know if I'll have time to see you holding your own babies, but I don't want to leave you alone." She puts her hand up when I open my mouth. "Don't give me that spiel about our employees being your family. This is weighing on my mind, Caleb. I want to tell your mum and dad I did alright by you."

Granny's been onto me to get married for years, but she's never mentioned my parents. It's only been six months since my car accident. Seeing the state I was in then and now finding out she's sick must have taken a toll. There's strength in her eyes; I know she'll fight this, but I can no longer deny I'll probably only have a few more years with her. If I'm terrified, she must be feeling a million times worse.

I nod.

"You'll get married?" Her voice rises with excitement.

I take her hands in mine. "Yes."

"I know a few nice girls I think you'll like."

"Whoa, hold on. I can get myself a wife."

She looks at me uncertainly. "Can you?"

I think about that question as I head back to Blossom Ford, in a small private plane owned by Cooper Beauty Industries, three days later. I can't have an actual marriage, but I want to make Granny happy. That only leaves a marriage of convenience. It's not unheard of in the circles I move in to set up a contract marriage for mutual gain.

Over the years I've heard of some elite matchmaking agencies, but Tiana's face popped into my mind as soon as the idea of a contract marriage formed. She said she needs money; she might consider my proposal. In return, I'll have a wife who'll be discreet, but so warm-hearted Granny will fall in love with her.

CHAPTER FOUR

Tiana

"HOW IS YOUR GRANNY?" I ask Caleb. He called last night and asked to meet today.

"It's stage four cancer. She's trying to be strong, but she's worried. On top of that, she's anxious about me."

"You're doing well. If you carry on improving at your current rate, it won't be long before you walk unaided," I say when he stops talking and stares at me with an assessing glance.

"That's not her biggest worry. She wants me to get married."

"You're one of the most eligible bachelors of Garnet City. That shouldn't be a problem." I'm proud of the way my voice comes out, light, as if I'm not jealous of the prospective bride. I wonder if Caleb wants me to help organize the wedding. Or maybe he'll be shortening his physical therapy contract with me. He was supposed to recuperate in Blossom Ford for two months.

"I'm not looking to get hitched for real. So, a contract marriage is my only solution."

I frown. "You mean like a marriage of convenience?"

"Yes. Where both parties gain something."

"I see." But I don't. And why is Caleb talking about this with me?

"You mentioned you're saving up to invest in your own business. I've seen how driven you are and the way you keep working at something until you get it right; I like that. Your honesty about how money is important to you is great. I believe you're the type of girl Granny would love." He interlaces his hands on top of his knees and I follow the movement, dazed by what he's just said. "Are you interested in entering into a contract marriage with me?"

I gape at Caleb; unsure I heard him correctly. I bite my lip to stop myself from jabbering. "Are you saying you want me to be the bride in your marriage of convenience?"

"Yes."

The way Caleb says it makes it sound so simple. He's looking directly at me, cool as a cucumber, while my head is spinning. I'm glad I'm sitting down.

"I'm not sure how long the marriage will last. I'm initially looking for a three-year period with the possibility of extension on agreement by both of us. The pay is one million dollars a year plus expenses and of course, you'll be able to carry on working weekdays, with the understanding you'll have to attend enough social events to make the marriage seem real. There would be other issues to consider, but we'd have everything laid out in a contract. What do you think?"

"I'll be back in a minute, just going to get water." I force myself to walk steadily, as if I'm not beside myself over what he said.

In the kitchen, I open the freezer and stick my head in. I stay like that until I've completed three sets of counting to ten. I get a bottle of water and down half of it. Only then does my heartbeat return to its usual rhythm. Being away from Caleb's mesmerizing eyes and that beard I want to pet helps.

I make myself go over what he said calmly, thinking about this as a business. With three million dollars plus my savings, it'll be easier to open a practice. The fact I can still work is also important. I won't be able to take on anything like I did with Caleb, but I can cover a few private appointments a day. I'm already contracted to work with Caleb for two months, so I'm not letting any clients down.

It all makes sense, but I'd be living with Caleb. My heart races again. I need a little more time to think. Besides, I can't agree with anything until I've seen the rest of the terms of the contract.

I finish the bottle of water and return to the living room. Caleb is still sitting where I left him.

He watches me until I'm sitting down. "Have you decided?"

"Can I see the rest of the contract first?"

"Good girl!"

The approval in Caleb's voice melts my heart and brings heat to my face. My freckles must be standing out, but there's nothing I can do about it, so I cross my legs as if his compliment didn't just shake my world.

Caleb picks up the briefcase on the floor and pulls out a set of papers. He stands up and walks the short distance to me, holds the papers out and watches me take it. It's taken effort to walk without the support of crutches and his brow is a little damp. My heart swells with admiration and respect for him all over again, and I know I'm already well on my way to falling deeply in love with him. That's why, from a non-financial point of view, this marriage of convenience might not be a good idea.

As soon as he's sitting down, I rush back to the kitchen and grab a bottle of water. Back in the room, I hand it to Caleb, then sit down to peruse the contract. I almost choke when I see sexual relations as a clause in the document. It's permissible as long as both parties consent to it.

"It seems okay. Can I have one night to think about it?"

Caleb agrees.

I think about it for the rest of the day. It's on my mind as I talk to Mum over the phone. She's living the life she's always dreamed of, with her new Greek husband on a small island off the coast of Greece.

I turn in bed most of the night, but in the morning, as I take in my small, rented studio, I make up my mind.

"You've decided," Caleb says as soon as he opens the door, standing with the support of two crutches.

"I accept."

From that moment, everything speeds up. That afternoon, we fly to Vegas.

"Shall I hire a dress at the chapel? I'm guessing your grandma will want to see a photo of the wedding. A wedding dress will help convince her we wanted to get married," I say in the private plane flying us. I don't hide the fact that I'm enjoying the experience of comfortable seats and not having to wait in line at the airport. I'm sure this is what Cinderella must have felt like when the coach appeared at the wave of a wand.

"It's taken care of."

I sip expensive champagne to help with the butterflies somersaulting in my stomach. Deciding to take things as they come, I leave Caleb to the work he's doing on a laptop and sit back.

In Vegas, we are whisked away to a hotel in a chauffeured car. There, two women are waiting for me with a wedding dress and make up set. They help me get ready. Once they finish, I stare at the stunning, sophisticated woman in front of the mirror. The white satin dress is simple and trainless, but it fits me perfectly like it was made just for me. I'm sure my resume didn't mention my dress size, so I'm not sure how Caleb knows my size so well. My long black hair is swept up in a stylish bun, with a few curls falling down the sides of my oval face. Even my freckles appear cute.

"Ready?" Caleb asks after staring at me for what seems like ages, when I open the door to my hotel bedroom.

I nod. I've never seen him in a suit. He is handsome in a tailored three-piece pin-stripped suit. He trimmed his beard too.

He wheels his chair round and I follow him to the elevator, through the hotel lobby into a car waiting outside.

"This is Daniel Thorpe. He's my executive assistant and friend," Caleb introduces me to the man waiting there. Daniel is almost as tall and wide as Caleb with sun kissed skin and a direct but friendly gaze.

They work the brief journey to the chapel. I sit facing them. They are the two most gorgeous men I've ever seen, and it takes some self-restraint to not stare at them. Instead, I gaze at the streets of Vegas and admire the late afternoon scenery. It's my first time here and I don't know when I'll have the chance to come back.

Less than two hours later, Caleb and I are married with Daniel as a witness and are on the private plane, heading back to Blossom Ford. There, after getting into Caleb's car, I must have fallen asleep because I suddenly come to when I hear him calling me.

"Are you awake?"

"Yes."

He helps me get out of the car. If he keeps being sweet like this, I don't know how I'm going to let him go when the contract is over.

"I'm flying out to Garnet City early in the morning. Granny's being discharged. Have a good rest," he says outside one of the guestrooms in his mansion, which is now my bedroom.

I clutch my bag because his blazer is folded over the back of the wheelchair and he's looking even sexier in his white shirt and waistcoat. I want to sit on his lap, kiss the hell out of him and touch the muscles that bunch every time he expertly turns the wheels on his chair.

"You were amazing today," Caleb says.

I blink. His voice is deeper than usual. His eyes are darker, too. He's staring at me so intently my heart speeds up. Then he breaks the spell.

He turns the wheelchair and wheels it away quickly. "See you tomorrow," he calls out.

CHAPTER FIVE

Tiana

CALEB'S BEEN AWAY FOR two days. He's coming back today; with his grandma. So I'm moving into his room, as per clause eight of our contract, that states we'll sleep in separate rooms unless something happens that requires us to sleep in the same room in order to make the marriage believable.

If it were my grandmother, I'd want her to convalesce with me too instead of with a caregiver. So, I'm a little nervous but I like that he's doing the right thing by his granny.

I hear the purring sound of a car and rush to open the door. Fall night air makes me shiver.

Caleb wheels his chair to me. "Hi sweetheart. Come here." He stretches his hand out to me and when I place mine in his, he pulls me down to his lap.

I'm ready for this; Caleb warned me we'd be acting for his grandma. But I'm not ready for the way my body ignites when his fingers caress the soft skin of my nape. Or the way he ever so slowly pulls my head down, brushes my lips with his, then nuzzles my nose.

"Miss me?" he asks when he pulls back.

"A lot." My voice is croaky, I'm surprised I managed even that.

"Come and meet Granny." Caleb nudges me toward an elderly woman that looks so much like him, I realize he takes after his father's side of the family.

"Tiana, I like you already. Call me Granny. Can I hug you?"

She reaches out and I wrap my arms around her gently.

"Did you bake? I think I can smell cookies," Granny says after Caleb has seen the chauffer off and we're inside.

"I hope you like them," I say.

"I'll eat them tomorrow. I can't believe how exhausted I am after only a thirty-minute flight."

"Shall I help you get ready for bed?" I ask.

"I can manage. You should be off to somewhere exotic. I'm already feeling guilty for intruding in your honeymoon, but Caleb insisted. Now, go. Do newlywed things."

Caleb chuckles and although I blush, I can't stop my lips from tugging up.

I stop outside the room. "Do you want something to eat?"

"I had dinner."

He heads towards his room, and I follow him. Inside, he swaps the wheelchair for crutches.

"I can sleep on the floor," I say.

"The bed is massive. It'll take both of us, unless you really want the hard floor."

I shake my head. I wash up first and get into pajamas in the bathroom. As Caleb takes turns washing up, I get into bed, pull up the covers.

He's wearing a t-shirt and soft pants when he comes out of the bathroom, his brown hair slick from the shower. He gets into bed and switches off the bedside lamp.

"Goodnight," he says.

"Goodnight," I answer. It's a long time before my eyes close.

When I wake up, something heavy is on my tummy. Before I see what it is, I realize I rolled into the middle of the bed and so has Caleb. A slight lift of the cover shows the heavy weight is his arm.

"Do you want me to take my arm off your body?" He asks.

I turn to him. Caleb's eyes are closed. His voice is thick with sleep and something else. Then his eyes open and I fall into them.

"No. I've been thinking about this since the day I met you."

"About what?"

"You touching me. What about you?" I can sense he's attracted to me, but I have to hear him say it. I don't want to be the only one burning. Don't want this to just be a morning crave.

"Sweetheart, I've been thinking about kissing all of you since that day, too. That's why I was such a dumbass."

A few beats later, he's still staring at me. "What are you waiting for?" I ask uncertainly.

"I want you to be sure."

My heart melts. I put my hand on top of his and move it towards my tits.

"Fuck Tiana! Do you know how much I've thought about touching these?"

I moan as he squeezes them. Then he sits up and switches on the light. "Stand up and take your clothes off. I want to see you."

I shiver at the command in his voice. I stand facing him and slowly take off my top then trousers, his eyes never leaving mine. My panties are getting wet and I'm a little embarrassed.

"Take them off and put them here." He extends his hand.

It turns out I enjoy being watched and commandeered. Another shiver runs through me. I take my black thong off, excited by the expression in his eyes. When I put it in his hand, he takes the panties to his nose, still watching me, and inhales.

"You're gorgeous, Tiana. So fucking beautiful I've been getting off thinking about you. Come here."

I'm dripping wet now, but I don't care anymore. I get in beside him.

"Lie on your back with both your arms stretched above your head."

When I've done that, he undresses, watching me the whole time. I break away from his gaze to stare at him. His chest is as beautiful as I'd imagined it. His rigid cock is reaching up toward his belly. I gulp.

Caleb stretches beside me and kisses my nose. I giggle.

"I love this pert nose and the freckles living here."

"Is that the first thing you wanted to touch?"

"Hmmm." Then his lips are on mine and he's kissing me, softly at first, then deeper until I'm gasping for breath. My arms move of their own volition, toward the back of his head.

"Arms back." He pulls them away and puts them back above my head. "It's been so long. If you touch me, I'll be finished. I won't last long as it is." There's an endearing, self-deprecating tone to his voice.

Caleb palms both of my tits, licks the nipples. I moan. "Fuck woman, I could worship your body the whole day. Harder?"

"Yes."

He nips them and I undulate, ready to have him inside me. He lets go of my breasts, slips one finger into my pussy.

"I'm ready." My voice is hoarse.

"For what?"

"For you to fuck me. Now."

He moves on top of me, then groans. "Shit, I want to come inside of you so badly, I forgot the rubber. Can you feel how ready I am for you?"

"Yes." His pre-cum is slippery on my thigh, mixing with my own juices.

He rummages in the bedside drawer, finds a condom, and slides it over his enormous shaft. Then he kisses me. We both cry out as he penetrates me. Caleb sets a pounding rhythm that is just what I'm craving and after only a few more thrusts, I wrap my arms around him as I come, my pussy strangling his cock.

He groans out his release and buries his head in my neck. When he's still, he rolls over until I'm lying with my head against him and his arms are around me.

I glow inside, remembering him telling me I'm beautiful. When I was in high school, I used to be so conscious about my body image, worrying all the time I wasn't as slim as most girls around my age. I did every type of diet I could find. In senior year, when one of the school's popular boys asked me to senior prom, I was over the moon. It wasn't until prom day I found out it was all a prank and he'd asked someone else to be his proper date.

After that, I swore to myself I'd let no one hurt me because of my body. If others would not love me, I was going to love myself. I ditched all my diets and, with time, learned to love myself as I was. It was funny how being self-confident actually made me more attractive; more guys in college started asking me out. I didn't need to hear the adoration in Caleb's voice, but it gave me a warm fuzzy.

CHAPTER SIX

Caleb

"GRANNY, YOU'RE CHEATING," Tiana laughs one evening.

Just like her voice, the sound is like music; it soothes me, makes me feels like everything is alright in the world.

"How is that cheating? Honestly, young people these days don't know how to strategize," Granny grouses, but I can see the twinkle in her eyes.

We're playing monopoly in the sitting room. The pitter patter of rain sounds from outside and, together with the fire I made, makes the room cozy. I reach for my mug of cocoa and sip the hot, sweet drink. Tiana makes hot chocolate the way Mum used to make it, with marshmallows.

I hadn't had hot chocolate for decades. Yet, the other day when Tiana was making it, the whole downstairs smelled of it and instead of sad memories, I remembered the fun I used to have with mum and dad. Tiana reminds me so much of Mum.

Two weeks have passed since Granny came to stay. Every day, Tiana has found something for us to do. Whether it's playing games, watching old movies or baking. The house feels warm and bright. Like it used to when I lived with Mum and Dad in Blossom Ford. I'd forgotten the happiness of those innocent days.

Every night, we fall asleep holding each other.

When Granny is tired of playing, we say goodnight to her and tidy up the sitting room. Tiana hates washing up, so I wash the cups while she dries. Leisurely, we head to our bedroom, hands intertwined. I started holding Tiana's hand for Granny's sake. Now it's a habit.

We make love and fall asleep, but a couple of hours later, I wake up, hard for her again. She's sleeping. I slide down the bed, gently part her legs and lazily tongue up and down the length of her clit. It's not long before she's pushing against my tongue. I keep the same pace, enjoying her sweet and tart taste.

"Caleb," her voice is thick with sleep. She runs her hands through my hair, stroking me there and even that makes me hotter. "Don't stop. Ahh, so good…"

"Come for me Tiana!"

She comes apart, her cry raw, "I love you Caleb."

I freeze. My chest tightens. I have to get away.

Tiana has fallen asleep. She's beautiful, but right now, I can't carry on looking at her. After dressing, I grab my phone, crutches and creep out of the house. I call a taxi and head for the airport. I get a first-class ticket and fly to Garnet City.

At around four in the morning, I arrive at Garnet City's Gentlemen Club. It's a member only facility that caters to the wealthiest men in the world. The place is buzzing with men playing cards and drinking. I nod to a few but head for the back room, where it's quieter and I can drink in peace.

"The usual, sir?" a waiter I recognize asks as soon as I sit down.

"A bottle."

I down the first couple of doses in one go. Tiana's words won't leave my mind. The fear they invoked is still squeezing my heart. Because I wanted to say those words right back at her. Don't really know how I stopped myself.

All these years, no woman has ever stirred my heart. I thought I was immune to love. I should have known something was wrong when Tiana was the only woman I wanted to consider for the marriage contract. Deep down, I wanted her to be mine.

"You don't look like you've found answers at the bottom of that glass."

I look up to see who's disturbing me when it must be clear I want to be alone. Blue ripped jeans and a black leather jacket are all I need to see to know it's Alexander Livingstone.

"Ginger." The nickname slips off my tongue. I've been calling Alexander that since we met in Junior High. We got off on the wrong foot; it wasn't until later we became friends. By then, we were too used to our nicknames, and they stuck.

"Lass," Alexander answers and sits down. His red hair is styled differently than the last time we met.

Only Alexander could think of naming me with that ridiculous noun. He is the respected director and heir of Livingstone Enterprises, a family owned multi-billion-dollar empire, but every time I see him, I can't help thinking he should live somewhere in the wilds of Africa or Australia. He said my eyes are as pretty as an Irish girl's, hence Lass.

"Do me a favor and leave me alone, will you?"

"Nah. I'm too curious. The only time you looked like this was when you thought you'd never walk again." He looks around and behind me. "You've ditched the chair. I'm impressed."

I knock back the contents of my glass and pour more. Forcing the mountain of a man in front of me to leave is pointless. "Congratulations on your forthcoming marriage."

Alexander scowls. Pours himself a drink and knocks it back. "You know it's for the merger between our two families."

I'm glad I'm not Alexander. As the CEO of our company, while I was growing up and learning the business, Granny was strict with me and always had high expectations, but I never for a moment thought she'd disown me if I failed to meet a goal she'd set. Things didn't work like that in Alexander's family.

"So, what has you hiding? You know I'm a good listener. And I always come up with solutions."

I smile at that. "I think I've fallen for a woman." The words sound strange to me.

Alexander whistles. Gives me a look of commiseration. We drink silently for a while.

"It looks like you're going to be miserable if you're away from her. At least together, you might have good times even if things go south later."

I stare at the golden liquid in my glass. If something were to happen to Tiana, what would I regret more? The pain of losing her or never loving her?

I'd hate myself for not telling her she's the only woman I want to spend the rest of my life with. I'd hate myself for not saying I love her. Even as I think this, I realize I've known it for a while now. I was just scared shitless to admit it.

I stand up. Reach for my crutches. "I'm going back to Blossom Ford."

"Say hi to August for me. I heard he got married. There's something about that small town and weddings. My future wife is from there too. And your mum."

"Maybe there's hope for you then."

August, Alexander and me were always together in college.

Alexander grunts. A beat passes. "You're the best man, by the way."

That is so like him. Although I don't feel like it now, among us tree friends, I'm the most sociable. Alexander doesn't talk unless he has to.

We go in different directions outside the club. It isn't possible to use the private plane right now and commercial flights are getting busier, so I head to a hotel to sober up before I return to Blossom Ford later.

CHAPTER SEVEN

Tiana

IT'S TWELVE O'CLOCK AND I haven't heard from Caleb. I'm worried sick about us. When I woke, there was a note on my bedside table saying, "going to Garnet City". At first I didn't worry too much about it, but then last night came back to me. The part where I told Caleb I love him.

Technically, there isn't an us. We're simply having fun with each other while our contract lasts. In reality, I've been falling in love with him. With the way he treats Granny like losing her will take away some part of him, the way he's so focussed when he works, his indomitable will to overcome his disability. I feel cherished when I'm with him and his way of loving my body, well, it literally makes me lose my mind and say things I don't mean to. I even love chatting with him. Sometimes we stay in bed chatting about life.

I'm mad I said those three words that could rip us apart, but I couldn't help them. The question is, should I pretend it was a mistake? The contract clearly states we'll go our separate ways after the marriage is void. I wasn't supposed to develop feelings for Caleb. He was clear he wanted to remain a bachelor for life. Wearing my feelings on my sleeve will strain our relationship.

I slide a tray of chocolate chip cookies into the oven. This is the third batch. Earlier, it was oatmeal and banana.

Thinking about the ingredients for the cookies distracts me. It would have been easier to keep myself occupied if Granny were here. But she left before lunch to meet Penny, an old acquaintance she'd met while visiting Blossom Ford when Caleb's parents were alive. They were having their hair done at Raven's Hair Salon and were going to Jackson's Diner after for a late lunch.

Caleb's car comes up the driveway. I wait for him to come in. I get the cookie jar and slowly put away the cooled banana and oatmeal cookies. When he reaches the kitchen, I'm just finishing.

He stands in the doorway and looks at me. He's too far away for me to make out what he's thinking.

Looking at him helps me decide. I want to stay with him as long as possible, even if I'm the only one loving. Even if Caleb doesn't say he loves me, his actions and the way his eyes find me whenever he enters a room, make me feel loved.

"I'm sorry," he says.

I blink.

He leaves the crutches by the door and stalks to me. For the last week, he's been walking around the house without crutches.

However, he's been on a long journey; I should assess the way he's walking, yet I can't think of anything else but the look in his eyes as he gets closer. It's making me feel owned. He reaches me and hugs me tightly.

"I can't breathe," I say after a while.

"Sorry." He eases up and I'm able to wrap my arms around him.

"What's the matter?"

Caleb pushes me back a little until he's looking at me, still holding my arms. "You shared your soul with me, but I left like that. I'm sorry, I was a jackass."

"You were honest. I broke the terms of our contract."

"You weren't the only one."

He pulls my hair back from my face.

"What do you mean?"

"I love you too, Tiana. Can you forgive me for the way I walked out?"

Caleb reverently kisses my temple. The gesture is so sweet warmth spreads through me. "If you apologize like this, it'll be difficult not to forgive you."

"That's what I'm hoping for. I had the hardest time getting over my parents' deaths. I even stopped talking. Losing people I love is something I don't do well with. My solution was not to get close to anyone. But you burrowed your way into my heart and now I can't live without you. Stay with me for as long as we both live."

"Oh, Caleb." I throw my arms around him, holding on tightly. "I will."

The oven pings, startling us. "Let me get the cookies out."

Caleb nips my lower lip before he lets me go.

"Where's Granny?"

"Out with Penny."

"Weren't they going to lunch? What time will they be back?"

"Around three, I guess."

Caleb comes up behind me, circles my waist. "We have plenty of time."

"For what?" I love teasing him.

His arms snake up my sides, and he squeezes my breasts. My smile disappears. Then he nips the soft skin between my neck and shoulder and I shiver.

He lifts the sides of my long, loose knitted dress and exposes my bare ass. "Good girl."

When he first told me to ditch panties at home, I was a little unsure, especially with Granny there. But she would never know and the way Caleb was so considerate of her, we did nothing where she might walk in on us. Which meant we always made love in the bedroom. By the end of the first day, the nerves had gone. My only concern was having a wet patch on my clothes.

Caleb kneads my ass and runs his hands up and down my thighs. I wrap one arm around his neck and turn my head to kiss him. It feels so right, the way our tongues duel together.

"Ahh, Tiana. I can't get the taste of you out of my head."

"Me too."

He rolls a nipple with one hand and with the other rubs my clit until I helplessly gyrate against him, moaning as shocks of pleasure spiral through my body.

"I love the soft way you feel against my hand when I touch you here." He gently slaps my clit before he's rubbing it again, faster this time.

I want to tell him I've always loved shaving down there, but all that comes out of me is a strangled yes as I convulse against his body, his arm holding me steady across my tits.

I'm still pulsing when Caleb leans me forward and nudges his cock against my pussy. I widen my stance, urging him.

"I want to come inside you."

"I'm safe." I press against the mushroom head of his cock and sigh when he buries himself to the hilt with a single thrust.

I wrap my arm around his neck as he fucks me leisurely, pulling almost all the way out before ramming back in and playing with my breasts until a fire is raging in my belly all over again.

"You feel so good, Tiana. Tell me you love me," Caleb growls against my neck.

"I love you."

"Put your hands on the counter," he rumbles.

As soon as my hands touch the surface, he grabs onto my hips and pounds against me. It's just what I need. I feel more juice come out of me, slicking Caleb's thrusts. He reaches round my hip and rubs my clit twice.

I come with a cry, arrows of pleasure shooting through every corner of my body. Caleb barks out his own release as he bucks against me.

"Are you okay?" Caleb's voice is rough from our lovemaking.

Concern has me standing upright. His recovery is progressing so well I don't want him to do any damage. "And you?"

"Let's sit before I make a fool of myself by collapsing. I think my legs will give out soon."

EPILOGUE

Caleb

One Year Later

FEAR IS A BULLDOZER crushing my heart. My hand is white, but I welcome the pain Tiana's crushing grip is producing. It means she's with me.

"Push," the midwife says.

The baby is a week early. This terrifies me, and I try hiding my overwhelming fear from Tiana, but it's useless. I'm looking at her and breathing with her, trying to avoid an all-out panic attack.

We take a deep breath and this time, when Tiana bears down and pushes, a cry sounds in the room. Tiana falls back on the bed, eyes closed.

"Are you okay?" My voice is so small.

I clear my throat to ask again, make sure she hears me, when she opens her eyes, smiles tiredly and squeezes my hand. She looks towards our baby, now swaddled in towels.

The midwife puts the baby in Tiana's arms. "Congratulations, you have a girl."

"Hello Emily Rose," Tiana whispers, then looks at me, her chestnut eyes shining with joy. "Look at our baby girl. She's perfect."

My chest is so fucking tight, I can't speak. The side of my face is strange until I realize tears are rolling down my cheeks. I dash them away and kiss Tiana on her cheek. Sitting beside her on the bed, I gaze at our baby girl. She's the tiniest human I've ever seen; my heart fills and I know I'm going to do everything in my power to protect her.

"Here, hold her."

Tiana places Emily Rose in my arms. I make sure my elbow is supporting her head, just like I learned in pre-natal class with Tiana. Emily opens her tiny mouth and blows a strawberry. "Hello Strawberry," I say, smiling at her.

Tiana laughs. "You can't call her Strawberry."

"Why not?"

She shakes her head. "Let's see what Granny and Mum say about it."

"She's beautiful." I can't take my eyes off her.

The senior midwife approaches me. "Let me wash her and then your family can visit."

"I'm going to sleep for a bit," Tiana says.

I hold her hand while the midwives check on her, the baby, and tidy up the room. When they leave, they place Strawberry in my arms.

"I didn't know you'd look so handsome blowing strawberries, Mr. Cooper."

Heat spreads up my neck. "I thought you were sleeping, Mrs. Cooper." Tiana still looks tired. I hold our little girl to her. "I think she smiled at me."

She just shakes her head. "She's too young for that."

A knock sounds before the door is opened.

"Where is my namesake?" Granny says as she and Tiana's mum enter the room. Rose is Granny's first name. Granny cried when we told her if the baby were a girl, we'd name her that. I stand back as the older ladies fuss over Tiana and Strawberry.

I don't know what the future holds for us. All I can do is be stronger for the women in my life. Nine months ago, when we renewed our wedding vows in front of granny and my mother-in-law, I promised Tiana I'd live each day as it comes, that I wouldn't let my fear that something might happen at any moment prevent her from living life fully. I cheer her as she works towards opening her practice. I even promised her the three kids she wants, even though childbirth terrifies me.

I am so grateful Tiana came into my life because now I know what living is. Every single day, I'm just going to provide for my family and love them with all I have.

MARRYING THE GRUMPY DIRECTOR

CURVY BRIDES OF BLOSSOM FORD BOOK 3

IRIS WEST

CHAPTER ONE

Alex

I KNEW THIS DAY would come. I'm only surprised by two things. First, that my father let me get to my early forties before laying the foot down and insisting I do my duty to marry well and produce an heir for our conglomerate. Second, that my so-called duty is a vision of the most luscious lips and tempting curves I've ever seen. If she weren't a daughter of a family with the same money-oriented values as mine, I might believe that duty might be sweet.

But Nia is a Weston-Parker. Her ancestor was a founding member of Blossom Ford. Her family's business empire of restaurants may be a little smaller than ours, but it is as classy as their regal blood. She looks like a princess and eats like one. We're having a family pre-marriage dinner at their Michelin Star restaurant in Blossom Ford.

Our eyes meet. Hers large and the darkest brown I've ever seen. She doesn't look away; for a beat, then another, before she puts the tiniest bit of steak into a mouth I'm already having fantasies about.

I ordered a background check on her and read the dossier. But the small picture attached to the tiny file doesn't do her justice. She is twenty-one; the file should have been larger. Most young people in my circle do drugs, drink heavily or have some other vice.

Nia's file is clean. She spends most of her free time with a friend, hanging at the ice cream parlor, going to the cinema and the occasional night out. But I know how influential families can hide dirt, so I'm not falling for the prim way she's sitting. I'm still a little surprised that on her second college summer break, she interned at one of our hotels and received an excellent evaluation.

"Let's toast the union of our children," my father says and picks up his wineglass. "To the prosperity of both our families. May Nia and Alexander be blessed with many children to carry on our union."

Our parents beam at each other. They arranged this mutually beneficial deal. We get the Weston-Parker's five-star restaurants in our luxurious hotels while they get to have a restaurant in a third of our five-star hotels across the world.

Nia lifts her glass in salute and there's a polite expression on her face, but she says nothing. She's a sacrificial lamb too. At least I've experienced the world, but she's fresh out of college. Even though arranged marriages are common in our circles, getting stuck to a man twice her age before having time to experience life fully must irritate the hell out of her.

"Why don't we let Nia and Alexander get to know each other?" Nia's mom says. Her eyes and glossy waves of hair are the only physical traits Nia inherited from her. She's slimmer and has that sophisticated look only mature women of the upper class carry.

Mother is older, but she's also slim and has that same air about her. "Alexander, why don't you take Nia to a bar? Somewhere you can have a pleasant chat." She looks at Nia. "Where's the best place to go, sweetheart?"

Nia glances at me before replying. "O'Connors, Mrs. Livingstone. It's not too far from here."

"Goodness, sweetheart! You're going to be my daughter-in-law. Call me Becky."

Nia smiles. It doesn't reach her eyes. But Mother has already turned to the vintage wine in her glass. I stand up, put my coat on, and watch Nia do the same.

"You're practically married. It's fine if you end up in a hotel room tonight." Nia's dad laughs and the other three parents join him.

"It's great to be young, isn't it?" I hear Father say as we move away from the table.

"Do you mind if we walk? The bar's only ten minutes from here," Nia says.

I shake my head. I don't understand the sudden urge to remove Nia from that room, where I know rude comments are being exchanged. Nia's parents are younger versions of mine, in looks, personality and values. I can image the bawdy conversation going on there. Though she must be used to stuff like that, I wanted to prevent her from hearing those jokes.

I thrust my hands deeper into my pockets. I can't do anything about the way my body reacts to Nia. That's biology. However, I can certainly control these feelings of protectiveness and empathy towards her. I'm not letting a woman into my heart again.

Though it's been thirty years, Mother's words are still as clear as the day she uttered them when I caught her making out with another man in our hotel suite, her bra strap half-way down her arm.

"What Mom and that man were doing is perfectly normal. Dad is doing it with other women. That's how the world is. Now, go back to sleep." She'd pushed me towards my room. I couldn't sleep and put a pillow over my head to escape the noises she and the man were making. What they were doing seemed wrong. I couldn't stop myself from thinking I had a bad Mom.

Years later, I learned what my parents did was a choice, but by then I'd stopped believing my family could be like the happy families in movies. I stopped hoping Mom, as I used to call her when I was little, would come pick me up after school like some of the other moms did. I stopped hoping for Sunday family picnics and got used to eating perfectly healthy meals alone.

Whatever this feeling towards Nia is, I'm stopping it before it takes root. Although Father is the CEO of Livingstone Enterprises, I've taken over most of his work for the foreseeable future while he recuperates from a heart attack. Thousands of employees depend on the success of our hotels and subsidiary companies. That's where my focus should be.

We walk quietly along Blossom Ford's Main Street, accompanied by the silvery moon, a gentle fall wind and the occasional shout from passersby exiting buildings. I make myself think about the new hotel we're opening in the West side of Blossom Ford, by the mountains, and focus ahead, away from the sway of Nia's hips.

"I'm sure you have things to do. Let's finish these drinks, then go our separate ways," I say after placing a pink gin and tonic in front of her at a corner table in the modern bar. O'Connors is buzzing with people from all ages and walks of life, enjoying drinks on a Sunday evening.

"I thought we could spend a little time together." She plays with the straw in her glass.

What does she mean? "Is there anything you'd like to know?"

Nia takes a long pull on the straw, her eyes facing the cup. "Not anything in particular."

"Did you read the marriage contract?" If there are any issues, I want to know now rather than later.

She sits up straighter. Tears her eyes from the gin and looks at me. "I did."

"Good. Do you want to wait a little before trying out for a baby? That's the only thing we have to decide on."

"What do you think?"

I'm used to people being intimidated by me, especially young women. But Nia doesn't cower from me. I like it.

Stop thinking about things like this, I tell myself. I can feel the frown forming on my brow.

"It's better to get it done. Then you can have your freedom." My voice is rougher than usual, but the thought of a little boy or girl wanting a hug from their absentee mom breaks my heart. No matter what kind of mother Nia turns out to be, I'm going to give my child all the affection in me.

She takes a moment to answer.

"I agree. There's a five-year term to fulfill the heir condition, but it's impossible to guarantee pregnancy. The sooner we start, the better," she eventually says.

God, the thought of getting her pregnant is making me hard. I drown the contents of my glass. "Are you ready?" Her glass is only half-empty, so I know I'm being a dick, even as I say the words. But I can't believe those emotionless words are coming from that kissable mouth.

"I'm done."

CHAPTER TWO

Nia

"STOP FIDGETING YOUNG LADY!" Mom says. She grabs my shoulders.

I look around the small room of the church, hoping someone will come rescue me. I don't want to have the talk Mom is about to give. Cause most of Mrs. Sarah Weston-Parker's talks are one-sided orders. I remember my best friend Jasmine went to get me a glass of water and sigh.

"Now listen. During the family dinner, it looked like Alexander was attracted to you. That is temporary. You must do everything to keep his attention. I saw you making eyes at him; I'm glad you find him attractive too. It'll ease a lot of things between you. I wouldn't mind marrying him myself, but never mind that." She looks up and down my body. "God knows I've tried everything to slim you down."

I swallow.

Mom shakes herself. "They've accepted the deal. Just keep his attention long enough to put a baby in your belly. Two would be even better. Keep counting calories. Go to Dr. Ellis if you need help. Stop wearing skinny jeans, they make you look scruffy. No affairs before you've had children. And for goodness's sake, don't forget what I taught you. Make sure you pay attention to what Alexander says about the business. Pass on any information that could be beneficial to your dad."

I nod. Arguing will only prolong this painful moment. Jasmine comes in, holding a tray with a bottle of water and four glasses.

Mom moves away. "I'll go see how things are in the church. Don't mess up your dress."

"You okay?" Jasmine asks as soon as Mom leaves the room. "Here." She hands me a glass of iced water.

"Thanks for coming in right then."

Jasmine has been my best friend since kindergarten. The only time we've been apart is college. We spent all our breaks together, making up for lost time.

"Did I mention you look fabulous?" she asks.

Laughter rips me up. "Ouch!" My dress is so tight, a tiny movement hurts my ribs. Mom ordered two sizes too small, hoping I'd lose enough weight to fit into it. But my body just doesn't function the way the rest of the Weston-Parker's female bodies do. Though I accepted it and got over it a long time ago, I can't help the way Mom and my twin sisters feel about it.

"The church is packed. It feels like the whole town turned up to see you off."

I blink. Twice. I'm going to miss going to Jackson's Diner for their raspberry ripple sundae, followed by movies on Saturday afternoons. On Sundays, I'll think of lazing around Blossom Ford Point and just chattering away the afternoon. And on Saturday mornings, I'll miss organizing play sessions with the children at the orphanage and making brownies with Mrs. Gallagher, the orphanage director. In some ways, since I turned fifteen and started volunteering at the orphanage, she's been more of a mother to me than my own Mom. "I'll visit."

"It won't be the same. I can't believe you're getting married. You're twenty-one. Who gets married at that age?"

"You know it could have been last year. At least I convinced Dad to let me finish college."

"That's your problem. How can you see a silver lining in everything? I would have run away by now."

"If I refused, Rosa would have to get married. She's only nineteen."

"Nineteen going on thirty. I know she's your sister, but she's as crafty and ruthless as your dad. She'd be fine with this type of marriage. Not you. You've always dreamed of having a home with a loving husband and a string of children hanging onto your apron."

I want to laugh again but restrain myself. I majored in hospitality management because it's what my family wanted. Although I enjoyed it, my heart is not in it. Not the way Rosa is. And even though I'm getting married to a man everyone believes is the impersonation of Grinch, I'm still hoping my dream will come true.

"It could be worse than Alex."

"Alex? Since when did you give him a nickname? I'm really worried. You've got a crush on your arranged marriage husband. Do you know how hard it is loving someone when they don't love you back? What if he has affairs after you have children? It's going to hurt."

"Maybe he'll fall in love with me?" I'm usually so confident, but even I am finding it hard to see how Alex could fall in love with an inexperienced girl like me with all the stunning choices available to a rich man of the world.

Jasmine sits on the sofa beside me. "If he has eyes, a beating heart and stomach, he will. Try making a home for him, the way you've always wanted to with your future husband. You have nothing to lose."

There is a knock on the door. It's Dad. Which means it's time. I smile to hide the jitters inside me, put my hand in the crook of his arm, and follow him.

Dad stops where the red carpet begins. Camera flashes blind me. Unbidden, my lips lift for the cameras, the way they've been trained to. The shares of our companies rose at the announcement of our wedding and the merger of some of Livingston and Weston-Parker Industries. By inviting the press here, Dad and Mr. Livingstone are doing everything to capitalize on that.

When Dad marches again, I look at Alex. He's six feet three inches tall, with adorable red hair and ripped muscles any girl could wish for. Almost everyone of my colleagues at the Livingston Hotel I interned at, was terrified of his temper, but the way he cleaned up the Livingstone Conglomerate and radically improved working conditions, made me believe he's a good man.

His deeply set cerulean blue eyes are on me. I latch onto them and march toward him.

Alex's hand is warm and firm in mine the whole time we say our vows. His eyes and voice are so steady, I want to believe he means them.

"Kiss your bride, Mr. Livingstone." There's laughter in the crowd. Father Ted is such a comic, but I'm in no mood to appreciate it today.

My heart is thumping at the way Alex is gazing down at my lips. He puts his hands around my shoulders and ever so slowly, lowers his head. His lips brush against mine, soft yet firm, sending pulses of electricity along my nerve endings. Before I can do anything, he moves away and I'm left wondering how I'm going to hide my crush, if I cannot get him to fall in love with me.

CHAPTER THREE

Alex

IT'S EARLY MORNING WHEN we arrive at our cottage at the Maldives Livingston Luxury Resorts.

"I have a meeting to attend. I'll be back at three," I say to Nia.

"Would you like coffee before you go?"

She yawned the entire way from the airport to here. Her hair is tousled from turning on the plane. She looks like she'll fall asleep on the spot. A spark of amusement ignites in my heart. I clench my teeth to stop myself from smiling.

"Get some sleep." I march to the bathroom and quickly freshen up. When I come out, she's on the sofa, fast asleep. This time, I can't stop my lips from tugging up. Nia looks like an angel. She tucked her hands under her head and her face is completely relaxed. I want to pick her up and place her on the bed but stop myself in time from doing such an unnecessary thing. The sofa is massive and looks as comfortable as the bed.

"Good morning, Mr. Livingston," the general manager welcomes me as I enter one of the hotel's meeting rooms, where a small group of staff is gathered.

I nod at them. He's one of my best managers; excellent at his job and doesn't waste time on trivial chit chat. Our luxury cottages have been so successful that we're building more on the land surrounding the main hotel building. While I'm here, I've planned to spend today and tomorrow checking out on the works and going over the overall running of the resort. The remaining five days of our honeymoon will be more than enough time for Nia and me to spend together.

"If everyone is here, let's begin," I announce then power up my laptop.

Nia is not in the cottage when I return. I change into swimming trunks, shorts and a t-shirt and head out to look for her. I could ask the hotel staff to help locate her, but I know how hard they work. Besides, I'm curious to see what she's up to. I head towards the pool bar first. It's just after three, the DJ is playing lively club music. The place is teeming with people lounging on pool chairs, drinking, swimming or dancing with the muscled hosts and pretty hostesses.

It takes fifteen minutes to work out she's not there. Thankfully, only a handful of staff try to greet me, and they quickly turn away when I glare at them. The message that I want everyone to treat me as a guest clearly went around.

She's not getting a massage or facial from some of the best beauticians the world has to offer in the beauty parlor, either. I recall the information in her file. She doesn't like golf, so I don't think she's at the range. I'm contemplating where to check next when a conversation between two staff members catches my attention.

"I heard you talk about Mrs. Livingston. Where is she?" I ask them.

Recognition sinks in and their welcoming smiles vanish.

"We're just getting back to work, Sir," one of them says.

"Mrs. Livingston?" I ask impatiently.

"Please follow me," the other woman says.

Screams and splashes of water get louder as I follow the staff member to the children's club. It's a large open area, with a roof overhead for rainy days.

Nia is sitting on a stool, laughing with a small group of children.

The staff member sorting out paints at the entrance startles, but I put my index finger to my lips.

As I get closer, I see the brush in Nia's hand and the face of the child sitting across from her. She dips the brush in paint and carries on the intricate design on the boy's face, talking all the time. I can't make out what they are saying, but it must be something happy; their laughter reverberates through the club.

Is this what she'd look like with our child?

Fascinated by the joy on her face, I move closer. Which is the real Nia? The young woman sitting daintily at the family dinner with a vacuous, polite expression or this bundle of happiness?

"Alex?" She stands up, dropping the brush. With awkward movements, she removes the apron she's wearing and apologizes to the next child in the line.

"I have to go, thanks for letting me help," Nia whispers to the member of staff that comes to take over her.

Outside the children's area, she stops. "I'm so sorry I wasn't there when you returned. I lost track of time. Have you had lunch?"

I nod. She's no longer flustered, calm and collected Nia is back. A dot of red near her mouth captures my eyes. My hand snakes out and wipes the spot. It takes a couple of tries to get rid of the paint. Then I notice her lips are slightly ajar and all thoughts of paint go out of my mind.

She's staring at me, her eyes a dark vortex. I dip my head, those tantalizing rose lips drawing me in.

"Will you be here tomorrow, Ms. Nia?"

Nia blinks. She turns in the voice's direction. "We'll see." She waves at the child, then turns back to me. "If we hurry, we'll make the snorkeling session."

I wait in the living room with a large glass of ice water while she changes. When she's done, we head out to the beach, just in time to join the snorkeling tour. Couples and families with young children fill the boat to capacity. Music blares off the speakers.

"Are you okay? It's a bit too loud in here, isn't it?" she asks me.

"When did you start snorkeling?"

"I think it was about when I was nine. The children's club at the hotel we were holidaying in organized a trip. I got the bug then. I've always wanted to do a snorkeling tour here, but it never seemed to happen. Thank you for agreeing to come with me."

"It's your activity." On the flight over here, Nia suggested we choose two activities each to do together during our five days. Out of a better plan for how to spend our time, I agreed.

"Are you an experienced snorkeler?" She asks.

"I've done a bit." Whenever my friend Caleb convinced me to visit some trendy beach spot.

When the boat stops, and Nia takes off her shorts and top, I nearly swear aloud. Her one-piece suit is the sexiest swimming costume I've ever seen. It hugs her stomach but leaves the sides of her chest and hips completely exposed.

Put your shirt back on, I want to say.

"Let's get in the water," I tell her instead, as soon as the guide finishes the safety demonstration. In the azure ocean, I steer her away from the other holidaymakers until we find a secluded spot where we can still see the boat.

I watch as she adjusts her mask and snorkel then put my own on. She points downward. I've snorkeled here and am familiar with the area, but her enthusiasm is so contagious, I see the coral and fish with fresh eyes. I show her some hidden spots too, and when we surface a smile of appreciation that reaches her dark eyes does something weird to my heart.

CHAPTER FOUR

Nia

MOM'S RESOUNDING REMINDER TO avoid jeans round Alexander repeats in my head, but he's already seen me in them. Besides, he's wearing ripped jeans that hug his butt and show his powerful thighs. I can't very well wear one of the formal shift dresses I brought. Mom is even more against the soft skirts I like to wear, so that's out of the question for tonight.

I settle on skinny black jeans and a smart casual top that suits me. This is our first proper dinner together as a married couple. I want to make a good impression on Alex.

As I slip on jewelry, I'm hoping he didn't hear me call him Alex, earlier in the afternoon. Later, when we know each other better, I'll ask if I can call him that. Another thought flitters through my mind. He never accepted my apology about not being here when he came back from work. But he didn't make a big deal out of it either. He smiled twice as we floated in the ocean. He was informative about the sea life here as well; it was fun to be around him.

I place a hand over my thumping heart. It's way too soon to be feeling like this. I should just be glad my messy face didn't irritate him. Dad and Mom hate mess. I still remember Mom's "Little girls don't play in the snow like that. It makes them dirty. So don't do it again," when my ten-year-old self couldn't resist the temptation to make snow angels one snowy winter.

It was the same with baking. Instead of leaving it to the chefs, I enjoy doing my own. Unfortunately, I'm a messy cook and baker. So, I stopped baking at home. I can only hope Alex is not like that. One of my dreams is to make as much mess as I want in my house before cleaning it slowly.

Remembering the way Alex looked at my lips heats my cheeks and makes me settle on the rose lipstick I was wearing instead of the red Mom advised. I spray my favorite perfume, slip into my lucky high heels, and head to the sitting room.

"You look gorgeous."

I smile as wide as a Cheshire cat, but I can't help it. "So do you. You look good with a beard." As soon as I've said the words, I look away, and wish I can take them back. Damn my blabber mouth. No matter how many deportment lessons I have, it still lets me down at crucial moments.

I muster the courage to look at Alex. He's looking right at me, a slight flush in his cheeks. I bite the inside of my cheek.

"Let's go," he barks.

I agonize over his tone for a few moments before the beauty of the Maldivian night sky and beach enthralls me as we walk to the restaurant. Anyway, I'm almost certain my compliment pleased Alex.

"It's breathtaking, isn't it?" he asks.

I nod.

As we are sitting by the window, I wonder if Alex asked for a table to be reserved because the restaurant is packed. It's not a Weston-Parker, but I've been to a few of their restaurants to know their food is almost as good.

"What are you thinking?" Alex says after tasting the wine he requested, and we've placed our orders.

I tear my eyes from the faraway place the sea seems to end.

"Living on a deserted island. As long as I have food, clean water and communication with the outside world, I think I'd love it." Damn my mouth again. What kind of thing was that to say to a savvy king of entrepreneurship? Mom would have a fit if she were a fly beside us.

Alex gazes at me as if he'd like to know the workings of my mind. Heat creeps up my neck.

"Me too."

"Really? What about work?"

He cracks up. It's a beautiful sound that has other women turning their heads in our direction. It's the first time I've heard it. The habitual frown on his wide forehead has disappeared and his cerulean blue eyes are full of mirth. I want to see him laugh like that every day.

"I work a lot, but that's not the only thing I do."

"I know you snorkel very well. What else do you do?"

He looks like he's not sure if he wants to share. I hold my breath.

"I hike. Seeing nature and the world from the top of a mountain is humbling. It's one of the best feelings in the world. At least for me."

From what I've learned about him, he's a very private person. I can't help wondering if he thinks he's shared too much.

"I've never tried it. I suppose you have to be very fit to do it."

"You can get fit hiking. It's like everything else. The more you do it, the better you get at it."

"Are you sometimes the only person on a trail?" It sounds wonderful.

"That's one thrill of it."

I'd love to share the beauty of nature with Alex, but I also understand his need to be alone. That's the type of person he is. No amount of grooming would ever change that desire to have time alone. Just like the thousands of dollars Mom spent on me, didn't change me from the ugly duckling she thought I was. I've accepted I can't influence her thoughts and hope one day she'll see I'm a princess in my own way. Just like Mrs. Gallagher said the day she found me crying at Blossom Ford Point after Mom lost patience with my "lack of progress in losing weight".

The waiter serves our dishes. I pick up my knife and fork, inhaling the delicious fragrance of a well-cooked steak. "One day, can I go with you? Not always, just sometimes. I think I'd love it. I promise, if I ever get to buying a small, deserted island, I'll take you to visit it now and then too."

He cuts up steak, pops it into his mouth and chews slowly. Then he nods and smiles.

Alex changes the conversation to my internship at his Chicago Hotel, but I'm happy to talk about anything. We've gone from eating and drinking awkwardly together to enjoying each other's company and dinner. That's progress.

The night sky is even more beautiful as we head to our cottage. I'm looking up when I trip over something on the sand. Expecting an ignoble tumble to the ground, I'm surprised when Alex stops my fall. I reach for his arms.

He pulls me up slowly.

"Are you okay?"

"Yes." My heart settles down after the shock of the near fall, then picks up speed again. The hairs under my hands are slightly rough. I want to rub my hands up and down his arms.

I'm so close to him my body is almost touching his. With the beach lights and the white of the moon, I can just about see the rapid rise and fall of his chest. I gaze up at Alex.

His eyes fix on my mouth. His head lowers and this time, I stand on tiptoe. I sigh when our lips touch. Alex pulls me closer, flush against him, and licks the seam of my lips. I wrap my arms around the nape of his neck and open for him.

He angles his head and strokes my tongue. I stroke back until our tongues are dueling. When I can't breathe anymore, I drag my mouth away. Alex licks up the side of my neck and nibbles my earlobe, sending arrows of electricity to my core.

"You're sensitive here," he whispers against my ear. I shiver. "Let's go back to our room." He takes my hand and leads the way to our cottage.

"I need the toilet." Why now, of all times? But I'd rather go than embarrass myself later. "I'll be back in a minute." I'm so embarrassed, I don't even look at him.

In the bathroom, I peel my pants down and sit on the toilet, ready to take care of business fast. A huge yawn is forced out of me. I only got a few hours of sleep after our flight; jetlag must be catching up with me. At dinner, I yawned a few times, but stayed alert. I shake my head. I can't fall asleep now. Tonight might be my lucky night.

I reach for the toilet roll and everything goes black.

CHAPTER FIVE

Alex

I WAKE UP TO Nia's soft body and a raging hard-on. She's still sleeping, her beautiful hands under her cheek.

Last night, after she'd been in the bathroom for a long time, I knocked on the door. When there was no response, I opened it, worried. Only to softly chuckle at the sight of her sitting on the toilet, head leaning against the wall, toilet paper in one hand.

She wouldn't wake up even when I crouched in front of her, gently called her name and stroked her soft cheek.

My heart stuttered, and I knew I wanted her to be truly mine.

I peeled her jeans off and carried her to bed. Though I was tired, I couldn't sleep. For the first time since I was a little boy, I wanted to have a proper family. Someone I could be vulnerable in front of, without worrying they'd take advantage or belittle me. I wanted to have children we could play with. Just like other families did.

I regret arranging a string of meetings for today. As quietly as I can, I get out of bed and have a cold shower. She's still sleeping when I come out. I dress and leave a note, saying what time I finish.

I get through the meetings as quickly as I can and extricate myself an entire hour before I'm due to finish.

"Call me if there are any other problems. We can't afford further delays in construction," I say to the general manager, and head back to the cottage.

Just before I reach it, I hear music. I unlock the door and push it forward gently. Only to freeze on the spot. Nia's head is thrown back in a dramatic pose as she belts against the back of a wooden spoon. I don't recognize the song, but I know she's not doing it justice. Her voice cracks here and there yet, her enthusiasm is contagious. It's the first time I've seen her in a flowing skirt. The soft material suits her.

I hum as she gyrates around the kitchen. There's a buttery scent in the air. Utensils and bits of flour are on every surface. She's been baking! I like to tidy up as I cook, but instead of getting annoyed, I smile. I've truly fallen for Nia. This irascible feeling wouldn't make sense otherwise.

"Alex!"

Warmth spreads through me. I enjoy hearing that nickname from her.

"You're back early." There's consternation in Mia's voice.

"Would I have missed your concert if I'd arrived on time?"

"What?" She puts the spoon down. "I'll get this tidied up straight away." She shifts utensils to the sink.

I stride toward the piling mountain of crockery, pulling my sleeves back. I open the tap, squirt in soap, and start washing the dishes.

"I can wash up. Your clothes will get dirty." She tries to push me aside.

"Let's do it together. I have other clothes."

I can feel her eyes on me as she wipes the kitchen surfaces and vacuums the floor. "I'm sorry about last night. And thank you for taking me to bed."

"It was my pleasure."

She ducks her head and picks up a drying cloth. She's so cute when she's embarrassed.

"Let the dishes air dry. It's hot enough." I dry my hands, the smell of delicious baked goods pulling me toward the tray on the kitchen island.

"These brownies look delicious. Can I have one?"

Nia comes and stands beside me. Watches me bite into the rich chocolate gooeyness.

"What do you think?"

I take another bite. Then stuff the rest into my mouth. "It's yummy."

She grins and I notice the spot of flour on her temple. I reach out and wipe it. Nia gives me a sweet peck on the cheek. But I've been wanting her so long, the innocent gesture makes me hard straight away.

I lift her up onto the island. Slide into the space between her legs. Then I'm kissing her, hard. I angle her head to get better access and moan into her mouth when her arms wrap around me and pull me closer.

"I've been wanting to do this since that dinner," I say against her neck. "I wondered if you'd look as prim if I kissed you. Touched you here." I knead a breast through her t-shirt.

"I've dreamed of kissing you since I was nineteen, when I first saw you. I," her voice breaks, "I made myself come thinking about you."

"God, Nia."

I tuck my hands inside her top and slide them up, past her uplifted arms. Then I unclip her bra and watch as her breasts are freed. I cup them.

"Look, they fit my hands perfectly." I lick the rosy nipples until they are tight and Nia is panting. Gently, I lower her down until she's lying on the island.

I trail kisses down her abdomen to her bellybutton. It's the cutest thing I've ever seen.

"Show me how you played with yourself."

"Now?" Nia's voice is breathy.

"Yes."

She slips her hand under the colorful skirt. I hook my thumbs under it and her panties and slip them down her beautiful legs.

"You're fucking gorgeous, Nia." I can't stop my eyes from roving over her voluptuous body. Already, my cock is straining against my pants.

"Now, Nia."

She closes her eyes.

"Keep your eyes open. I want you to see how touching yourself makes me feel."

She looks at me, then slides her hand past the dark curls on her mound until she's touching the engorged flesh between her legs. Using her middle finger, she rubs it up and down twice, then circles it and repeats the pattern, moving faster until she's panting.

I rip my shirt off.

"Let me finish you. I put her ankles on my shoulders and slide my hands under her butt and around her hips. With my tongue, I mimic the movement of her hand, licking up and down then round her clit, gradually increasing speed."

Nia undulates, pushing against my tongue. Then she cries out and convulses. When she stops moving, I hold her gaze. "You're mine alone Nia, do you understand?"

She stares back. "Yes, as long as you understand, you're mine alone, too."

I nod. Then rise and unbuckle my belt. The phone rings. "Hell and damnation!"

Nia giggles.

My lips lift in response. "I have to take this call."

Nia sits cross-legged. There's no way I can speak coherently while looking at her sitting so prettily. I turn my back and answer the phone. I almost curse as I realize I have to leave Nia.

"There's an emergency. I'll be back as soon as I can." I kiss her temple, drag myself away.

CHAPTER SIX

Nia

I SHOWER AND DRESS, singing the whole time. That was my most intense orgasm. I never thought I'd be able to touch myself in front of a man the first time we got together, but hearing Alex's words and watching his reaction helped my embarrassment disappear, leaving lust in its wake. But what made my day was Alex's promise. To be monogamous. I believe he'll keep it. That's the kind of man he is. He doesn't talk much, but when he does, his words are important.

I get out my tablet and settle down to read until he comes back. Mom calls a couple of hours later. I move to the backyard and stand by the pool, then answer the phone.

"Have you and Alexander done it?" She asks after we've exchanged greetings.

"Mom, that's private."

"If you're pregnant, you'll show. If not, you won't. There's no point hiding it."

"Pregnancy is not something I can control."

A laugh. "Just have more sex. You'll have a higher chance of conceiving. Now, what have you learned about the competition for the project I told you about?"

I swallow. "I haven't had time to find out anything. We're on our honeymoon; it'll look suspicious if I ask Alex about business matters that are not in the public domain. You said to gain his trust first, too. I haven't done that."

"Don't take too long. Your dad has other sources, but you live with him. Alexander practically makes all the decisions. If you could find out how much the other companies are bidding, it'll give us a significant advantage."

"I'll try my best." I hate having to spy on Alex. I'm just going to stall until Mom concludes I'm useless and stops expecting intel on the Livingston Conglomerate.

"What the fuck was that?" Alex growls.

I turn around to see Alex bearing down on me. How did he get into the house without me hearing? The only reason I went outside was to prevent something like this from happening. I thought that out here, I'd have time to end the conversation if I heard him come into the cottage.

He grabs my shoulders. "I said, what was that?"

He looks scary, but I know he's hurt because of my words.

"It's not what it sounds like. Let me explain." My heart is pounding.

"Well?"

I try to think. If I admit the truth, his relationship with my parents will sour. They are not friends, but at least there's cordiality between them. How can I tell him Mom asked me to spy on him? But I can't come up with any other plausible reason.

Alex turns away. I grab onto his elbow.

"I know how that conversation sounded, but it's all a misunderstanding."

"How is it a misunderstanding? Did you even mean the promise you made to me?"

"I did, Alex. I swear."

"Who were you talking to?" He growls.

"I didn't mean any of it."

He removes my hand from his elbow and marches off. I call after him, but he either doesn't hear or ignores me.

He doesn't come back for two days. I call his cell and leave a million messages. He has every right to be mad at me. He was opening up to me. Hearing those words must have made him feel betrayed.

I cried and berated myself for not telling Alex everything. I don't want to lose what we started to build. It was too special. But I don't know how to make things better without revealing the truth.

I'm walking on the beach to get fresh air and clear my mind. Maybe I can find a solution to the misunderstanding between

Alex and me. I reach a part of the beach I haven't seen before. There are a few quad bikes racing away from the main resort.

I'm about to turn back when I spot a toddler waddling towards the water. One of the quad bikes is on a collision course with the kid. I call out and start sprinting, my only thought to keep the child safe from harm. When I reach him, the bike is almost on us. I turn, putting the child in front of me, my back to the bike, and close my eyes.

CHAPTER SEVEN

Alex

WHEN THE GENERAL MANAGER informs me Nia's been involved in an accident, my heart drops. Fear for her petrifies me. Then I'm out of my chair, racing for the door of my temporary office.

"Take me to her!" I bark.

"The fastest way to get there will be a three-wheeler vehicle."

"How bad is it?" I don't care about the snark in my voice.

"I'm not sure yet, but I don't believe anyone's badly hurt. The doctor and first aider are already at the site."

I grip the side of the car. Thoughts of Nia pass through my head. Laughing as she face-painted, dancing in the kitchen and sleeping on the toilet. I haven't prayed since I was little, but I say a silent prayer, pleading for her safety. Because she's my life. I don't want to think about living without her.

I jump off the vehicle as soon as it stops. I sprint to her, relieved to see her sitting up, wrapped in a blanket.

"Nia." I crouch in front of her and hold her hands in mine.

"I'm okay."

"God Nia."

I pick her up and sit on the chair, crushing her to me.

"This is Doctor Prakez," the general manager introduces an elderly man.

"How is she?" I ask.

"From what witnesses said, Mrs. Livingston wasn't hit. There are no fractures or contusions on her body. She fainted from shock, so a little rest is all she needs."

"She doesn't need to be checked at the hospital? Have tests?"

"A rest will suffice," the doctor says quietly.

I want to take her to a hospital to be doubly sure she's okay, but I know the retired doctor is one of the best in the world.

"Alex, please take me back to the cottage. I'm really okay."

I inhale and exhale a few times. "Thank you," I say to the physician.

I stand up with Nia in my arms and sit in the three-wheeler vehicle, holding her until we get to the cottage. I thank the general manager, go inside and take Nia straight to bed.

"Are you okay? I am so sorry, Alex." Nia holds my hand when I sit beside her.

"What the fuck are you sorry for?" I stand up.

"I didn't mean to hurt you. Those ugly words were lies."

"Why are you worried about me when you could have lost your life?" I sit back beside her, yearning to touch her, to be sure she's alright. "Never put yourself in danger again. Do you hear me?"

When Nia nods, I lie down and pull her into my arms. Nia pats my shoulder and, after a while, I feel calmer.

"I'm the only person who should be sorry. I know what our families are like, the things we're forced to do. If I hadn't been scared shitless of losing what we have and actually made myself think rationally, I would have come to my senses earlier."

Nia looks at me. "Sometimes, especially when I was younger, I'd wish I was born into a regular family like my friend Jasmine's. I'd swap all the presents and expensive clothes for the hugs and laughter in that family."

I stroke Nia's back. "It's been a long time since I thought that, but I used to think that too." I take a deep breath. "Let's make our family like that. You, me and any children we have. Let's love each other and them, the way we've always imagined."

I wait. And wait. Nia lifts up and kisses me on the forehead.

"I love you, Alex. I want that too."

"I love you." I'm so choked up I'm not sure she understands what I'm saying until she smiles and lies back on my chest.

"I may not always choose Weston-Parker Industries for future projects, but I promise to care for your parents and siblings the way you do. I won't keep things from you either."

"I'm glad. Your fairness in business and the way you cleaned up Livingstone Conglomerate is one reason I fell in love with you. I don't want secrets between us."

Nia slowly traces my bottom lip with her index finger. My cock stands to attention.

"You need rest." I pull her finger away.

"I'm horny."

I roll with her until she's beneath me. "Okay, we'll take it slow."

Gently, I peel off her clothes. Then I stand up and rip mine, basking in her adoring gaze.

Back in bed, I kiss the corners of her lips. She angles her head and kisses me back, open-mouthed, driving me wild.

Her hands stroke down my back and cup my ass.

I bite her bottom lip. "There'll be no slow loving if you touch me like this."

"I want to touch you, the way you touched me. Can you teach me?"

I freeze. "Is this your first time?" My voice is as light as I can make it.

"Yes."

As softly as I can, I kiss her. I have to be extra slow. "I'll teach you next time."

I nibble on one earlobe, then the other. Then I leave a trail of kisses along her neck and on top of her breasts. I take my time caressing the large tits and rolling her already-hard nipples. Her moans make me harder, but I resist the urge to pound into her.

Slowly, I lick my way down her tummy and play with the curls on her mound. Following the rhythm she taught me; I stroke her clit. She's so pretty, like a flower.

"Don't stop, Alex."

I love her raspy voice. "Not until you come, Baby."

I slowly insert one finger into her dripping pussy, then a second, third, and fourth. I pull them until they are almost out before pumping back in repeatedly.

Her head thrashes from side to side. I use my free hand to rub her clit and fuck her harder and faster until she cries out and bucks against my hand.

I slide up her curves, kiss her deeply, and press my cock against her entrance. In one swift move, I bury myself to the hilt inside her and swallow her cry of pain.

She's so fucking tight, I almost lose control. I still, using every breathing technique I know to stop myself barreling into her.

"Are you okay?" Nia asks.

"Jesus, woman!"

"It's okay if you came. My friends told me it happens sometimes."

Laughter ripples through me, shaking my body. It's the first time I laugh during sex. "How do I feel inside you?"

"Full. The pain is gone."

"We're not finished," I say against her mouth. Then I move, gently at first, so she gets used to the stretch of having me inside her. "Wrap your legs around my ass," I order.

When she obeys and grips my shoulders, I thrust harder and faster, until all I can think about and feel is the sweet heat of her cunt. The moment I hear her cry and feel her sheath contract against my cock, I explode. A little later, when I can move, I wrap her in my arms.

"I want to do that again."

The shakes come back. "Right now, that's impossible. Also, if you don't soak your body in hot water, you might be sore later. So, let's rest a bit."

"I love how kind you are to me. I'm never going to leave your side."

"You're mine now. I don't let go of what's mine."

EPILOGUE

Nia

Two years later

"REMIND ME, WHY DID we get this mountain of a tree? I thought we said we'd get a smaller tree this year." I place a shining red bauble on the bottom layer of our Christmas tree. It's the first of December, the day we decided to decorate our house for the holidays. I'm sitting cross-legged in our cozy sitting room.

"You fell in love with it and refused to open your heart to all the other trees at the farm." Alex is decorating the top of the tree. He promised to make every first of December a family holiday and took the day off work.

"How long did it take us last year?"

"Tired already? Let's take a break. You've been sleeping a lot lately. Maybe we should see a doctor."

He wraps his arm around me, and we walk to the sofa. I lie down with my head on his lap. I love this position. We read like this all the time. Sometimes I'm sitting and his head is on my lap.

I still can't believe Alex likes cozy mysteries. I've always imagined he'd enjoy reading books about business and nature.

"I'm fine, but we'll need more presents next year."

Alex chuckles. It's happening more and more, but I never tire of seeing how it relaxes his face. "I bought you five presents already. You want more?"

I want to know what he got me. Last year, it was romance eBooks, a hiking trip for two and a dessert cookbook.

I put my hand on my stomach. "These little ones will need presents."

Alex lifts me up into a sitting position, faces me.

"Are you saying what I think you are? Did we make a baby?"

"Not a baby. Two babies."

"Twins?"

I nod.

Alex lifts me onto his lap and hugs me tight. I rest my head against his chest, feeling his thundering heartbeat.

"I wasn't sure and wanted to confirm it before telling you."

Twice, I thought I was pregnant and wasn't. Just in case, I didn't want him to be disappointed a third time.

"I'm so happy, Nia. Sometimes, when I look at you, I pinch myself to check you're not a dream."

"Me too."

"I don't know how to care for one baby. How will we manage with two? You're such a natural with kids. I know you'll be a great mom. What if I let them down?"

"You won't."

"How do you know?"

"Alex, you might be the grumpiest man I know, but you're also the kindest and fairest. Being a little afraid is a good thing. It just means you'll take care to love our babies." I pull back so I can look into his eyes. "I'm a little afraid too, but we can attend parenting classes together."

Alex nods.

I lay my head back on his chest. I love my job. Working for Weston-Parker Industries Charity Foundation gives me joy, but I'll have to work part-time after giving birth. I want to spend as much time loving our babies as I can.

I also love that although Garnet City is our primary home, we spend a lot of time in Blossom Ford. I can't wait to show our kids the beautiful places I grew up in and love so much.

MARRYING THE
POSSESSIVE NEIGHBOR

CURVY BRIDES OF BLOSSOM FORD BOOK 4

IRIS WEST

CHAPTER ONE

Jasmine

HOW THE HECK AM I supposed to choose between pistachio and strawberry ice-cream? I can't. So, I'm having both. Not at the same time; I hate that. With a bowl of pistachio ice-cream, I stroll to my cozy sitting room.

This is the life I wanted for myself after finishing my nursing degree; helping children get better when I am at work then having lazy downtime watching movies or visiting my favorite places. Mom and Dad are away on a cruise, so I only need to do the bare minimum where housework is concerned.

The only thing missing is a chef to cook delicious meals. Some days, when I've had a hard time at the hospital, it's tiring to cook. Still, there are instant noodles and it's way better than being married fresh out of college like my best friend Nia. A shiver runs through me at the thought of having to give up my freedom as I plonk myself on the plushy, leather sofa.

I hated watching my parents work so hard to take care of me and my sister. They married straight out of high school after finding out Mom was pregnant with my sister. They didn't experience adulthood without the responsibilities marriage and children bring. I promised myself I would travel the world and have fun before I had so many responsibilities.

Qualifying as a registered nurse was the first step toward my goal. In a couple of years, when I've gained enough experience, I can work all over the world and visit the places I've dreamed about.

The sound of a powerful motorcycle makes me pause. I hold a spoonful of ice-cream inches away from my mouth. Riding a bike is something else I'd like to do. It's a shame the bikers that came to town last year seem a little too scary for me to contemplate befriending them.

I finally place the ice-cream in my mouth and close my eyes, savoring the ice-cold deliciousness. I reach for the remote control, but before I turn the TV on, I hear what I think is the sound of a motorcycle shutting down. From next door.

I frown. It's Tuesday, the new owner is not moving in till Thursday. Besides, Mrs. Thatcher–the previous owner of the house and my neighbor of twenty-two years, said the new owner is a middle-aged writer. I jump off the couch and pull the curtain open a little.

My heart beats a little faster when I spot a large motorcycle parked on the front lawn of the neighboring house. I'm five feet ten, so I'm used to tall people, however the man stalking toward the front door is large even to me. He's dressed all in black.

My heart sinks as he bends and does something to the door, his large back blocking my view of the keyhole.

I dial Mrs. Thatcher's number. After the fifth ring, I give up. Somehow, he opened the door. I run to the kitchen, look around for something, anything I can fend off the man if he becomes aggressive. I can't think of anything. The frying pan I used in the morning catches my attention. I grab it and my keys and head next door.

I try to quiet my pounding heart. It's hard to know if my footsteps are silent. Before I open the gate to the house, I dial 911.

"He's lurking around in the darkness. He would have switched on the lights if he were here legitimately," I whisper into my phone when Cal, the young police officer I went to school with, asks if I'm sure it's an intruder.

"For heaven's sake, Jasmine, just go back home and wait. I'll be there soon."

A noise sounds from the inside, like a vase falling and smashing into smithereens. I can't stand out here any longer.

In the yard, I lean down and take a close picture of the bike's plate. Then I creep towards the door, the frying pan held high. I slip past the open door and meet darkness. No wonder the intruder is breaking things.

I debate whether to switch the light on my phone but decide against it. That might alert the thief. Because only one would skulk in the darkness like this. I know the layout of the house very well; it's the same as mine. Swearing noises come from the kitchen, so I head there.

I can just make out his back when I enter the room. He's pointing his phone torch into a cupboard. I move away from the kitchen door, leaving plenty of room for him to run away. Although I'd love to catch him, my safety is more important. I just want to make sure he steals nothing.

I switch on my phone torch and aim it at him with my left hand. With my right, I lift the frying pan and wave it threateningly.

"I called the police. You better leave." I tried strengthening my voice, yet even I can tell it's trembling.

Instead of running, he points his phone towards me. Moves it up and down the length of my body.

"They'll be here any minute now. The police," I say, tensing up, fear a bitter taste in my mouth that sours even more when he moves toward me.

"Don't come any closer." I take a step back. And another, mirroring his movement.

He stops. He's even taller than I thought he was. There's an air of strength and agility in the way he moves. The room feels smaller. Is that a smile on his face?

"A Goddess just walked into my house. How am I supposed to keep still?"

I blink. Have I stumbled into a madman? How can he try to flirt with me in such a situation? Does he think I'll fall for this type of sweet talk? Or that I'm bluffing about the police?

"If you don't stop, I'll hit you," I say, brandishing the pan.

"Stay still and put the pan down. Let's talk. The floor has a few shards of glass."

As if I'm going to listen to him. I take another step back. He moves forward. I swing the pan with all my might. Instead of the satisfying thud and yelp I expect to hear, I spin until a powerful arm presses my front flush against the intruder's solid chest.

My breath whooshes out and I sense the frying pan fall from my nerveless fingers. I try to move away, but nothing happens.

"I'm going to marry you. I will not hurt any bit of these beautiful curves," his voice is a seductive whisper against my neck.

I shiver, unsure if it's from fear alone. Appalled, I try to move out of his arms again.

"I'll let go. I'm not a thief. This is my house."

"Then let me go."

He releases me. I rush away from him and trip over something. My leg gives way. I fall, hard. I hear a shocked expletive before pain jars my body and I see stars dance.

CHAPTER TWO

Hunter

THE MOMENT I saw Jasmine, I knew I found the woman I'd been searching for all my adult life, since the moment I decided I would not live alone like Mom. Jasmine's beautiful curves, full lips and shining locs drew my eyes, but I knew for sure when I saw the determined look on her face as she confronted me. She was smaller than me, didn't know what I might do to her, however she was willing to protect a neighbor's house from someone she thought was a thief.

That's when I fell for her and knew she was supposed to be mine. I never expected to find the woman of my dreams brandishing what she thought was a weapon against me in a darkened kitchen. Or for her to be so young. She's seventeen years younger than me. I learned this when the police officer she called and I checked Jasmine into the emergency room at Weston-Parker General Hospital.

"Mr. Wilson?"

I glance at the young police officer. "Everything checks out, so you're free to go. I'm sorry for the misunderstanding."

I nod at Jasmine. "It's my fault she hurt herself. I'll stay until a family member comes."

"The thing is her parents are away at the moment. I could call her friend or sister, but I don't think she'd want that, not when they live out of town, and it looks like it's nothing too serious. I'll call or pop in when I can to see how she's getting on."

There's more than a concerned cop to citizen relationship between Officer Thomas and Jasmine. There's something in the way he says her name that rings alarm bells inside of me.

"Do you know her well?" I ask.

His eyes drift to the bed where Jasmine is sleeping after he stares at me for a while. He's a few inches shorter than me, but he's bulkier, with a bodybuilder's physique. He looks about twenty-four. "We went to school together. I know her family well, too."

I like the younger man's steady gaze, however; I hope I'm wrong about my suspicions regarding the way he feels about Jasmine.

"I insist on staying."

"She might be a little shocked if she opens her eyes and sees you sitting there. She doesn't yet know you're not a thief."

"I'll get a nurse or doctor straight away."

Officer Thomas gives me another assessing glance, but when his radio beeps, he eventually nods, speaks briefly to a couple of nurses at the nursing station, and leaves the Emergency Room.

I sit back in the chair facing the bed, savor the sound of her name, let my eyes rove over her oval-shaped face, pert nose and beautiful dark brown skin. Her locs are black close to her head, then golden brown at the tips.

Her eyes open. She blinks at the ceiling twice before she looks around the room and her gaze lands on me. Recognition returns. She tries to sit up, winces and lies back. I get Martha, the nurse who'd asked for my autograph earlier.

"Hi sweetheart. Officer Thomas brought you in. You fell? You have a few bruises on your arms and face and your body might be a little sore, but you have broken nothing. We're just waiting on a few results and if everything is fine, you can go home."

Jasmine picks up the remote control beside her and elevates the bed until she's in a sitting position.

"Do you remember what happened?" Martha looks at me, then back at Jasmine, who nods. "Officer Thomas said to mention he's confirmed Mr. Wilson here is the owner of the house next door." Her lips tug up. "You're so lucky to be living next door to such a famous writer. I'm jealous, to be honest."

Jasmine looks at me. "Writer?"

"Oh my gosh. You must not like thrillers. Mr. Wilson is one of the best phycological thriller authors in the world. And he's one of our own." She pushes her white hair behind her ear and looks at me.

"Thank you, Martha. I'd really appreciate if you kept the knowledge that I'm in Blossom Ford a secret for now."

"My mouth is a tomb," she says a line from one of my books.

I'm still humbled by how many people read my books. I started getting used to large book signings in New York, but when people began recognizing me on the streets, I knew it was time to leave and find a quieter place. Of all the places I've been to, none in the US are quieter than Blossom Ford. So, I returned home.

Martha looks at Jasmine. "Let me know if you have questions. Also, if you'd like us to call anyone for you." She checks the observations machine beside the bed, writes something down on the patient notes and moves to the next bed.

"I'm sorry. The new owner is not supposed to move in for a couple of days, so I thought you were a thief. You must have been shocked," Jasmine says.

Her eyes are nearly black. They are huge and dominate her entire face. "I freed up my schedule so came early."

"Why were you moving around in the dark?"

My face heats. I shrug. "I couldn't remember where the electric board was. But it looks like the electricity is turned off, anyway."

The doctor that examined her earlier approaches the bed. "Jasmine. I'm doctor Jamal Stone. Glad you're awake. You have a mild concussion and some bruises. If you have someone to keep an eye on you for the next twenty-four hours, you can go home tonight."

He looks up from his notes.

"I do," Jasmine says.

My eyebrows shoot up.

"Good. Regarding the soreness in your body, just rest for a couple of days, take some painkillers if you're in any pain. It should sort itself out. Same thing with your sprained ankle. Just rest it." He smiles. "I heard you work in pediatrics, so you know the score."

"Thank you, doctor Stone," Jasmine says and watches him leave with a spark of admiration in his eyes, before she turns to me.

Slowly, I inhale. The measured action helps me control the jealousy that flares up in my heart.

"Once again, I'm sorry for the trouble I caused. Thank you for coming to the hospital. I guess I'll see you around, since we're neighbors."

"I'll take you home."

Jasmine's smile doesn't reach her eyes. "I'll call my parents. They'll pick me up."

I sit back in the chair. "Aren't they away at the moment?"

Her eyes narrow. She crosses her arms. "Right, I forgot. It must be the fall. My sister will come. I don't want to trouble you any further."

I sit back up. "Jasmine. I don't think your sister is in Blossom Ford either. Or any of your close friends. I'm sure there are people you can call. Blossom Ford is a small town and a few people in the hospital seem to know you, but I don't think you'd want to bother them. Your cop friend said he'll check on you, however I'm guessing he's busy at work and can't stay with you, otherwise he'd be here."

Her arms tighten even more.

"You can't be on your own for a day and I work from home. I feel bad you got hurt. The house owner said she'd tell the neighbors about me, so I think you know a little about me. She definitely told me about the nice family that lives in the adjacent house. She used to take you to kindergarten?"

"Why would Mrs. Thatcher tell you about that?" She ducks her head and reaches for the glass of water on the table beside the bed.

All I'd been interested in was the fact there were no young children in the neighboring house, but now I'm glad part of me was listening to Mrs. Thatcher's gossip.

"I also need a place to stay. In the morning, I can get the electricity switched back on or buy candles. I'll be working the whole night, so I just need to use a kitchen. We don't need to see each other if you'd prefer it that way. Just tell me you're okay now and then. You can also tell your cop friend what's happening."

Jasmine stares at me. Then she nods.

CHAPTER THREE

Jasmine

BRIGHT LIGHT HITS MY windows. I know it must be around nine, but I don't want to open my eyes. The smell of coffee causes my nose to twitch.

I bolt upright. Pain lances through my ankle and I remember my humiliating fall. Even more humiliating apology to Hunter Wilson. Seriously, how was I to know he'd pushed forward his move? Moving around in the darkness was also suspicious. At that time of the night, how could I think about something like the electricity being off? Mrs. Thatcher could be a miser sometimes.

He must be making coffee. And something else. My nose twitches again. Bacon, eggs, and sausages. If I were as good at cooking as I was at smelling food, I'd have gourmet meals every day.

I locate the crutch the hospital gave me and gently get out of bed and head to the bathroom. I take care of business and wash up. When I hobble out, Hunter is waiting for me.

I'm grateful I'm leaning on a crutch. It's the first time I'm seeing Hunter in good lighting. His widow's peak, hawked nose and sharp features make him attractive; I can't help staring. Until I realize he's checking out my whole body.

I stand with my legs apart, place the crutch in front of me, and fold my arms. "Stop looking at me." Last night, in hospital, I was dazed by the fall but now I remember him flirting.

"I'm a first aider. I'm making sure, as far as I can, that you're okay."

"You are? A first aider, I mean?" Jeez, I can't even talk properly. What am I, a high school junior having her first crush? Only I don't remember being this embarrassed when I crushed on Cal.

"Yes. I worked as a lifeguard for a while. I haven't updated the certification in the last few years, still I keep up on it as research for my writing."

He stretches his hand. I gaze uncomprehendingly at him.

"Crutch."

"I need it."

"Your ankle will heal faster if you don't put any pressure on it."

Then I remember. Him carrying me upstairs last night and asking if there was anything I needed. When I shook my head, he'd asked where my pajamas were and didn't leave until I told him and he'd placed a pair on the bed beside me. All in the name of not straining my ankle.

"I'm better this morning. If I'm careful, I should be okay."

Hunter looks at my swollen foot. Then he takes out the crutch from my fingers and places it against the wall. As if I weigh nothing, he picks me up.

"Get the crutch."

"I could have walked," I mumble, but he doesn't seem interested in what I'm saying. He marches downstairs and deposits me in a chair at the kitchen table.

"Coffee? Or would you like something else?"

I want to refuse yet it smells so good, I nod. I'm starving as well. So, when Hunter places a full breakfast and a steaming mug of wonderful smelling black liquid in front of me, all I can do is thank him.

I watch in silence as he serves his own food, tops up a mug he seems to have been using, and sits across from me.

He's still dressed in black, a long-sleeved t-shirt and jeans that fit his body like a glove.

I'm struggling over the fact that he's a writer. How can someone who sits down for a job have such an athletic body? His rugged good looks, longish hair and the way he walks make him look more like a member of a motorcycle club.

I stop myself from moaning at the flavour of the eggs. They are good enough to rival even Mom's. The bacon and sausages are cooked just the way I like them too, well-done but not burned.

"What are you thinking?" He asks.

"Are you a member of the biker club that turned up in town a while ago?"

"No. There are a couple of clubs I'm friends with. Sometimes I ride with them. I heard there's one in town."

"You've never wanted to join?"

Hunter pauses, like it's a question he wants to consider thoroughly. "I've been tempted, but I guess I'm too much of a loner."

I remember what I heard about his family. "I heard you mom still lives here, and you bought the Irwin place for her."

"I guess you know a lot about me, enough that I can start courting you properly."

Coffee goes down the wrong pipe. I cover my mouth as a coughing fit makes my eyes water. Hunter passes me tissues.

"Are you okay?"

"I will be if you stop saying things like that."

Hunter pours me more coffee.

"You're a beautiful woman. I'm just letting you know I like you and want to marry you."

I go hot all over. Put my cup down. "We've only just met!"

One side of his mouth tugs up. "You have heard of love at first sight, right?"

Why does that half-smile make him seem cute and playful? I shake my head and tell myself to concentrate. Hunter Wilson is too good looking for his own sake.

"I'll admit you're handsome in a rough way, but even if I wanted to date seriously, there's no way I'd get married now. I'm only twenty-two, for heaven's sake! And you can't blurt things like that. You keep it to yourself until you know what the other person is thinking."

Hunter pushes away his empty plate and stares at me with steepled fingers. As if he's trying to figure me out.

"What do you want to do before you get married?"

There's such an earnest look about him, like he really cares. "I want to travel the world. I've only just qualified and started working as a nurse. Once I've gained enough experience, in maybe a year or two, I plan to work in other countries and get to know the world that way. It won't cost too much then."

"How would marrying me stop you from doing that?"

"Seriously? How can I traipse around the world if I have someone else to worry about?"

Hunter shrugs. "I can write anywhere in the world. I love traveling too. What places do you wanna see?"

"Remote places," I lie.

"They sound great. I've been to some of those places. Wouldn't mind going again." He sits back in his chair, eyes on me, as if saying what else?

"I've finished. Thanks for cooking breakfast." He's so cocky, I don't want to admit how good the food is, however my sense of fairness wins.

He insists on carrying me out of the kitchen. This time, I don't bother arguing. Maybe because of that, for the first time, I'm aware of every single part of skin our bodies touch - the strength of his arms where they hold me, the barely there sensation of his hair touching my hands as they rest on the back of his neck.

I glance at his neck to distract myself and find something fascinating there, too. His Adam's apple is so pronounced I want to touch it.

It's a relief when Hunter deposits me on the couch. "Thank you." My voice is husky. I cough to dispel attention from how hoarse it is. I get Netflix ready. Nothing distracts me like a great film or drama. I'm getting all thoughts of Hunter Wilson and his cocksure ways out of my head. His answer about being able to work anywhere makes way too much sense.

CHAPTER FOUR

Hunter

AFTER I'VE SETTLED Jasmine, I wash the dishes. I can't help thinking about our conversation. At twenty-two, I was still finding my way in the world, working every job that would take me to survive and send some money to Mom in Blossom Ford. If someone had suggested marriage, I would have told them to fuck off.

It wasn't until a couple of years later when I met Linda and Henry Franklin that I realized how beautiful love between two people who were fated could be. Till then, I'd always seen Mom struggle on her own to bring up me and my sister Eve. We were dirty poor even though Mom seemed to spend all day waiting tables.

Linda and Henry run a coffeehouse/reading library in Garnet City. Customers could read the books there for free while they drank coffee and ate the pastries Linda was so good at making, but they couldn't take the books home. Each wall of the building had shelves stacked to the brim with books the couple had bought or received as donations.

That's where I discovered how much I loved stories and that I could do something about the tales that had always formed in my head. Henry was a retired teacher who loved books and teaching. He found me reading a psychological thriller one day during my break and started asking me questions about what I loved and would improve about the book. Apparently, the writer was one of his favorites. At first I was annoyed. The man was my boss. I didn't want to socialize with him during break times, yet it wasn't long before I started looking forward to our conversations.

I'd always hated school and barely graduated high school before I left Blossom Ford, still I couldn't wait to talk about stories with Henry, as he insisted I call him.

Linda loved feeding people while Henry adored coaching. They weren't lucky enough to be blessed with children. They welcomed all lost souls like me, who crossed their path as family.

The doorbell rings. "Stay where you are. I'll get it," I say when I spot Jasmine reaching for her crutch.

"Morning." Cal is standing outside in his uniform, which is now rumpled.

I move aside and close the door after him.

"Cal, what the heck are you doing here? You just finished your shift," Jasmine says.

"Jas, I'm hurt. Do you really think I would have gone home without checking on you? I can stay if you want me." He glances at me, then turns back to Jasmine.

"I'm perfectly fine. Thank you for checking up on me and calling last night. Now, go home and sleep."

He hands her a bag of what looks like doughnuts.

A grin splits her face. "You know me so well. Thank you again."

"Call if you need me."

Cal turns to leave and I uncoil myself from the door to the sitting room where I've been standing, watching them. I'm sure now the cop has feelings for Jasmine.

After I wave the cop off, I go to the kitchen and call the electricity company. Then I sit down with my laptop to work, but thoughts of Jasmine enter my mind. I give up. I'm way ahead of my deadline for the current book I'm working on anyway, so I'm not worried.

"Do you mind if I join you?" I ask her.

"Don't you have work?"

"I worked through the night."

"You can sleep. I'm fine."

"It hasn't been twenty-four hours yet. Besides, I'm used to going for a couple of days without sleep to complete a deadline."

"When this is finished, I'm switching to a romcom."

My lips tug up. I sit down on the chair closest to the couch. "I get lots of ideas from romcoms."

"Are you able to watch a movie for fun or is your mind always analyzing the plot and searching for ideas to use in your books?"

"I've always loved movies and dramas that tell a good story. I still get involved in the drama, but you're right, I can't help noting things down I can use in a book. So, even watching movies is a little like working. My readers say my characters are emotionally complex. I think that's a direct effect of watching romcoms and romances."

"I suppose you watch them with your girlfriends."

"My mom and sister."

She looks at the screen. I force myself to glance away from her and do the same. When the credits roll, I realize nearly two hours have passed.

"You can choose the next film," Jasmine says so grudgingly I can't help chuckling.

"Are you worried you'll hate my choice or you're one of those people who likes to hog the remote control?"

"Both."

I chuckle again and settle deeper into the chair. She's not getting rid of me that easily. "You can choose."

It's the kind of movie Mom and Eve like to watch. When Jasmine cracks up at a funny scene, I watch her and my heart stutters. The joy on her face is contagious. It warms me up.

At lunchtime, I throw some sandwiches together and we eat them in the sitting room, with the glazed doughnuts as dessert.

She insists on helping with dinner, so I carry her back to the kitchen.

"Where did you learn to cook?" She asks as she chops onions while sitting on one of the chairs at the small kitchen table.

"Mom was at work most of the time and would leave sandwiches or leftovers for us. Sometimes I fancied something hot, so whenever I could, I watched her cook. Once I learned a few dishes, I took over the cooking. I improvised a lot, so Mom and Eve, that's my sister, suffered a bit."

"Your mom was probably glad of the help." She smiles at me. "You must be the older sibling. My sister is ten years older than me; for a while she did most of the chores when I was little."

"Evie's younger," I agree.

I pick up the chopped carrots, wash them and put them in the pot of bean soup I'm making. It's a quick, nutritious dish that only takes half-an-hour to make.

"You're an excellent cook! This is delicious," Jasmine says after a mouthful. "I wonder if it'd taste as good if I make it."

"We can do it together until you get the hang of it, when your foot is better."

She asks me a question about a movie we watched earlier. And that's how we end up talking about movies for the rest of the evening until she dozes off.

I pick her up and head for the stairs. She's warm and soft and awake.

"I like your Adam's apple," she says just before we reach the toilet.

I freeze. She traces her fingers down my throat and I feel it all the way in my cock.

"Jasmine." I can't help the growl in my low voice.

Her eyes leave my neck and collide with mine.

I lower my head and do what I've been wanting to do since I saw her at my place.

I kiss her.

Her lips are soft against mine. I nibble her slightly fuller bottom lip and her arms tighten around the back of my neck. I lift my head and stare at her. Her eyes are darker, and her lips are slightly open. This time, she's ready for me and kisses me as hard as I kiss her until we're both breathing hard.

I kiss her temple and place her on the floor outside the toilet, feeling the glide of her hands as she releases the back of my neck. Then I take a step from her. Because if I don't, I'll want so much more.

"I'll hobble to my bedroom when I finish."

I make sure she's safely inside the bathroom before I go down the stairs, wondering if Jasmine's injury and the happy family pictures dotted around the entire house will be enough to fight the temptation to walk into her room and make love to her.

CHAPTER FIVE

Jasmine

"HOW IS YOUR FOOT?" Hunter asks in the kitchen as he places a bowl of porridge in front of me a few days after the accident.

He's wearing a thick, black turtleneck sweater paired with black jeans. It's criminal how good he looks.

"Pretty fine, considering I just walked down the stairs for the first time since the accident."

Hunter moved back to his place on Thursday and spent most of his time putting away belongings the removal company delivered. His electricity is back on too. Yet, he's spent every mealtime and evening at my place.

"You're glad right? If you'd put pressure on that ankle going up and down the stairs, you wouldn't be walking as well as you are now."

He's right, however, I'm out of sorts and he's the reason for it. I'm in no mood to admit how his superb care of me helped me recover. Because while I'm well physically, mentally, I'm a wreck.

I don't know what possessed me to touch Hunter's Adam's apple that night. That episode ignited a passion I didn't know I had inside of me. During the day, I listen out for the sound of his voice telling me he's letting himself into the house and at night; I dream of him making love to me. I've only known him for a few days, yet I already love the sound of his laughter, the way he taps his fingers when he's deep in thought and watching movies and dramas with him.

I would never have considered myself a psychological thriller reader, but after I asked about his writing on Thursday, he signed a book and gifted it to me. I totally surprised myself yesterday when I picked it up after lunch and was engrossed in it when he came in the evening to make dinner.

"Are you sure about returning to work tomorrow?" Hunter asks.

"I'll take my crutch just in case." There are some great-looking male doctors and nurses at the hospital. I need to be among them to see if what I've started to feel for Hunter is caused by close proximity. Maybe if I'm away from him, I won't crave him as much as I do now.

"Let me do the dishes," I say when we finish eating.

"I'll be back in a couple of hours. Make sure you wrap up." He looks at me, then lets himself out.

He has said nothing more about me being the woman of his life, though his gaze makes me feel branded. The tension between us is almost palpable. I'm glad I convinced him I'm well enough to go for a ride because I'm not sure I can be in the house with him without embarrassing myself by jumping his bones.

I bristle as Hunter checks me out before he deems I'm adequately wrapped, but deep down there's a warmth that has nothing to do with the layers of clothing I'm wearing.

"Are we ready?" I can't hide my excitement as he starts the bike after checking my helmet and putting on his own.

It's mid fall and there's a brisk wind in the hair. I hung on to Hunter and feel it whip my locs back as the powerful bike eats up miles of tarmac. It's as exhilarating as I thought it would be, and when Hunter switches off the engine at Blossom Ford Point, I'm a little sad.

I stand under the blossom tree and spread my arms wide, breathing in the pure cold air and scents from the vegetation all around me; and the river that runs through Blossom Ford Point. My boots crunch leaves as I slowly make a full turn.

The sound of a camera going off makes my eyes open. Hunter snaps another picture with his cellphone.

I roll my eyes and stick my tongue out, the way I do for the kids at the ward. He snaps another picture, laughing.

Sometimes, I can't believe Hunter is thirty-seven years old. At moments like this, he seems so much younger.

I take one side of the blanket in his hands and together; we spread it on the floor. I peer into the picnic basket he made. There's a small bottle of wine besides the sandwiches, fruit, pots of yoghurt and water bottles.

"I bet you were prom king your senior year." I sip wine and watch him gulp back half a bottle of water.

"The opposite." He closes the lid on the bottle. "I hated school and had anger issues. I think I disliked not being able to help mom and had a chip on my shoulder about accepting charity. Some of my clothes were handouts from my friends' moms."

"Kids can be cruel."

"True. Nevertheless, it wasn't their fault Dad became ill and passed away soon after Evie was born. Once I got my head screwed on properly, I could appreciate the kindness of the Blossom Ford Community, however interfering they can be."

I laugh. "I hate how everyone gets involved in everyone's business. But I never want to live anywhere else, not long term."

"Me too," Hunter says softly, gray eyes on me.

My heart skips a beat. He's staring at me as if I were his prey. He leans towards me, plucks a purple leaf out of my hair.

"You're beautiful with this on your hair, by the way."

I lean over and do the same to him. "So do you."

"I want to kiss you."

"What are you waiting for?"

He kisses the corner of my mouth, but I want more. I turn and angle my head for a deeper kiss. He slides his tongue into mine and pushes me down onto the blanket. Sighing, I glide my hands through his hair.

It's amazing to have his body stretched out on top of me. His hands rove up and down the sides of my torso and hips.

"You smell so fucking good," he murmurs along my neck, dropping tiny kisses there.

I pull his head back to my mouth, unable to get enough of him. His kiss is like a drug I've become addicted to. Each pull of his tongue sends electricity to my core.

His hand finally grabs my breast through layers of clothing and a coat.

"Yes Hunter," I moan into his mouth.

He freezes. Lifts his head.

"What's the matter?" I want to relieve the frustration I've been suffering the last few days.

"Someone is coming this way."

"What?"

But then I hear it. The sound of barking.

Hunter sits and pulls me up, tucking a stray lock behind my ear. "Let's carry on when we have some privacy."

I nod, awed by the way he cares for me. The chemistry between us is off the charts. I like so much about him; I think I'm falling in love.

CHAPTER SIX

Hunter

IT'S EARLY SUNDAY MORNING and I'm sitting in front of my doctor and friend Logan at his large private hospital in Garnet City.

"High tumor markers don't always mean cancer," he says.

"It may be."

"You're not experiencing any other symptoms, so the likelihood of that is very low. You must have a biopsy to know for sure. I can fit you in tomorrow, if you want it done as soon as possible."

"How long before the results are out?"

"I'll rush it. We should have the pathology report in a few days."

I wasn't expecting to be here; I think as I sit at a coffee shop after my appointment with Logan, unable to concentrate on work or anything else.

After our bike ride yesterday, I dropped Jasmine home and flew to Garnet City to meet my editor for a meeting regarding my next book. Before I arrived at our meeting point, I received a call from Logan asking me to see him at the hospital this morning.

I'd been a little worried. For the last five years, I've arranged for Mom, Evie, and me to have yearly check-ups. Apart from a callback for vitamins for Mom, Logan has never called any of us in. I didn't expect this.

Mom calls, but I mention nothing. She's visiting Evie. I don't want her or Evie to worry when this may just be a scare. Hearing Evie's husband and two boys in the background makes me smile.

I book myself into a hotel, but find it hard to sleep. After a night of tossing and turning, I crawl out of bed early and force myself to work, researching my next project. I want to hear Jasmine's voice, however the need to share what's happening with her is so strong; I can't take the chance of calling her.

The next morning, as I wait for the sedative I took for the biopsy to wear off, I wonder how cruel life can be sometimes. I finally found the woman of my dreams; yet, I might not spend my life with her because of cancer. There's no way I'd start something with Jasmine for her to suffer the way Mom did if I'm not around.

I fly back to Blossom Ford in the afternoon and take a taxi home. A cop's car is parked outside Jasmine's house. I wonder if Cal is inside when the door opens and the cop and Jasmine step out.

I get out of the taxi as Cal turns towards Jasmine, pulls her to him, and kisses her. Rage explodes inside me. I'm sprinting across the road and yard before I know it. Jasmine pushes Cal away a couple of beats before I reach him. It's not enough to curb my anger.

"Hunter..." Jasmine calls out.

I grab Cal and shove him further away from her. My hands fist. I use all the strength in me to stop myself from punching the younger man. Jasmine places her hand on my arm.

Cal grabs onto a post, his face ashen. He looks towards Jasmine. "I'm so sorry Jas. I don't know what came over me."

"I'll call you later," Jasmine says.

Cal looks to where her hand is holding onto mine, then turns and strides to his car. We stand on the porch until he's driven away.

"Are you okay?" I hold on to her shoulders and examine her. She looks a little dazed.

"Cal kissed me, I pushed him away. Nothing really happened."

"I saw it. Make sure you rest your ankle." I force my hands off her shoulders. "It's been a busy couple of days; I need sleep."

As I leave her house and walk to my yard, I can sense her eyes boring in to me. My head a mess, I grab a beer from the refrigerator and drink it in one go. I want to hug Jasmine, feel her warmth, and smell her heady fragrance. At night, I want to fuck her senseless, then sleep with her in my arms. I want to wake up with her and see all the places she wants to visit.

But how can I go to her now, when I might not stay in her life? Right now, I can't say I'll give her tomorrow, make any promises.

I grab another can of beer and down it quickly. When that doesn't destroy the wave of helplessness roiling inside me, I change into sweats and go jogging, setting a punishing pace. Maybe exhaustion will give me a reprieve from the anger and fear raging through me, even if it's only for a little while.

CHAPTER SEVEN

Jasmine

"GET A GOOD NIGHT's rest. You've been so distracted, if you carry on like this, you'll probably get a warning. You don't want that, not when you're still on probation," my colleague Sharon says as she drops me off after our shift.

"I will. Thanks." I wave her off and head to Hunter's place. There's no answer when I ring the bell. A string of curses slips out of me.

I take my phone out of my bag. There's no answer to the texts I sent him. No missed calls, either. His bike is in the yard, so he's not out riding.

The last three days since he walked off my porch, I've been mad. Even if he's tired or busy, he can still find time to send a quick text, surely. He admitted he saw what happened between Cal and me, so he must know I didn't kiss Cal back. He can't be angry about that.

Does he think I somehow encouraged Cal? Could he be blaming me for what happened? I shake my head and head home, completely at a loss.

When Cal popped in for a visit and confessed he was in love with me, I realized I'm in love with Hunter. I was scared that I had such powerful feelings for a man who's ready to settle down, yet I was excited too. Have I missed my chance with Hunter just like Cal missed his chance with me when I crushed on him in high school, but he wasn't into me? How could someone fall out of love in a couple of days? Perhaps what Hunter felt for me was lust.

I get out of my uniform, shower, and slip into comfortable clothes. I switch on the TV, but half of me is listening for movement next door. Because I'm starting to worry about Hunter. He's not the type to avoid things. If he's no longer in love with me or what happened with Cal is bothering him, he'd tell me.

It's only four o'clock, however it's already dark outside. I close the curtain, still, now and then find myself flicking it open to see if Hunter's back.

A couple of hours later, I hear a car and head to the window. Hunter's getting out of a taxi. I rush to the door before I realize I'm in my socks. Quickly, I get my slippers and dash back to the front door. Only to see Hunter letting himself through my gate.

Hunter spots me and stops. Then he bolts toward me and picks me up. I squeak in surprise and grab onto his shoulders as he twirls, laughing.

My lips tug up. Relief floods through me. Hunter is fine.

Why didn't he reply to my messages and missed calls then?

As he slides me down his body, a flash of desire hits me. Ignoring it, I take a step back.

"What's going on?"

Hunter gives me that assessing glance that seems to take everything in. "You'll catch a cold." He grabs my hand, pulls me inside, and shuts the door.

"Well," I say once we're indoors and all he's doing is stare at me.

"I love you, Jasmine Williams!"

I want to tell him I love him too. "You were gone for three days. You didn't answer any of my calls or text back." I move away from him and cross my arms.

"I'm sorry. I'm trying to figure out how to explain the fucked-up situation I was in."

He sits on the sofa.

"You went to see your editor in Garnet City?"

Hunter sighs. I've never seen him looking so lost. He doesn't look like he's slept much.

I sit beside him. Take his hands in mine. "You're scaring me. I need to know what's happening."

"My doctor called while I was in Garnet City. My checkup showed increased tumor markers. I had a biopsy. It's negative, but it took a couple of days to get the results."

A heavy weight settles on my chest. Did he go through this alone? "Did you know this when you came back on Sunday?"

"I wanted to call, hear your voice. I just didn't want you worrying."

"Did you at least speak to your mom and sister?" Even as I ask, I know the answer.

He shakes his head. Stands up.

"Loving someone means going through pain with them. It hurts me more that I couldn't be there for you. What if the result were positive? Would you push me away?"

I see the answer in the hard set of his shoulders. "Hunter, you can't make that kind of choice for me."

He turns to me. "I can't put you through what my mom suffered."

"We can't control what'll happen. We can only be there for each other with all our might. Has your mom ever complained about loving your father? Of course, she would have been exhausted a lot, however did you ever feel she regretted caring for you alone?"

Hunter looks struck.

I stand up and close the distance between us. "I love you too. But I need to know if something happens, you'll trust me to go through it together, just like I'd trust you if I were ill or going through a difficult situation. That's what marriage is. Living through the good and bad together."

Hunter stares at me for a long time, gray eyes dark. His Adam's apple bobs up and down. "I can try," he finally says.

I wrap my arms around his waist. "That's good enough for now."

"I love the way you smell. I missed it and you so much." Hunter's arms close around me.

"You look like you haven't slept in days."

"There's something I want more than sleep right now."

Hunter lifts my head and presses his lips against mine. Hard. And just like that, I want him. I angle my head for a deeper kiss, but he pulls back.

"Not here, with your dad looking down on us."

I laugh as he grabs my hand and leads me across to his house.

As soon as we're indoors, he pushes me against the door and presses his lips to mine.

His mouth is like nectar. I can't get enough of kissing him. Every pull of his tongue sends shockwaves to my core. I tilt my head, wanting deeper into him, and glide my hands up and down his chest.

He grips my sweater and slides it up my body. I duck my head so he can slip it off. Then he takes my bra off, releasing my large breasts.

He sucks one nipple into his mouth and fondles the other, rolling it into a hard point. I clutch the door, desperately trying to hold myself up.

Hunter pulls harder. It feels so good I can't stop moaning.

"I've been dying to kiss you here. I can't wait to get inside you."

"Me too. If my panties get any wetter, I'm going to embarrass myself," I rasp.

"God Jasmine," Hunter growls. He moves away from me and shrugs off his coat, tosses it to the floor beside my top, his gray eyes smoldering.

I push my trousers and panties down and step out of them, unable to take my eyes off Hunter as he crouches to untie his bootlaces.

Shit, I'm getting wetter just looking at him.

He shucks off his trousers and lifts me, presses me back against the door. I wrap my legs around his waist. Sense him guiding his cock against my dripping pussy.

We both groan as Hunter drives the round tip of his cock forward.

"You feel so fucking good." He bites my neck. "Are you okay?"

I grasp his shoulders and roll my hips, trying to hurry him. "I need you all in."

I tug his head to me and slide my tongue into his mouth, getting drunk on the dancing of our tongues. He pulls back his hips and rams back in, again and again, setting a fast pace until all I can think about is Hunter.

Every thrust is heaven and drives me higher and higher. He strokes my clit and I cry out. My whole-body trembles as my core clenches around his shaft, waves of pleasure rolling through me.

He stills and grunts against my neck. A jet of hot cum fills me, intensifying the sensations inside my pussy.

"You're mine, Jasmine."

I lay my head against Hunter's chest.

He kisses me softly. "I want to do this with you every day."

"Against the door?"

"Nah, my legs won't cope, not every day. Besides, I want to take my time, taste every bit of you before I fuck you slowly."

"I won't say no to that."

EPILOGUE

Hunter

Six years later

I FINISH THE LAST revision on my manuscript, press save and email it to my editor. I roll my neck and stretch my shoulders.

My phone beeps.

"Got the manuscript. I need you to stay in the UK for a few more years. Your fans are going crazy over the new series you're setting there."

I chuckle. "Roman, you know I have a family, right?"

"Your beautiful wife won't mind."

"I'll take lots of pictures. Just like I did in Qatar. My beautiful wife will be home from work any time now so, take care." I hung up the phone and stand up, just as a bark sounds.

I walk through the open door of my study, in the cottage Jasmine and I are renting, to the living room.

Our son Olly stands in his cot, arms pushing through the spaces between the bars to pet Baxter, our spaniel. He puts up his chubby arms when he sees me.

"Daddy!" He jumps up and down.

"Did you have a good sleep?" I carry him out and kiss his cheek before I put him on the floor beside Baxter, who's shaking his tail.

"Mommy," Olly says.

"Let's go wait for her."

It's early fall. It's already cold in Southeast England. I put a jacket over Olly's baby grow and a pair of sneakers on his tiny feet. The smell of the sea hits me as we step outside and I sit on the wooden bench in our front yard. Baxter runs around in circles and Olly chases him, trying to catch his tail.

I spot Jasmine and watch her run the rest of the way home. Baxter and Olly throw themselves at her, making her laugh out loud. She crouches and pets them until a seagull cries overhead and they stare up at it, pointing excitedly.

She comes and sits on my lap. I pull her closer and kiss her.

"We're going to scare Mrs. Green again," she says when we come up for breath.

"The next time we move, we're getting a house in the middle of nowhere."

Jasmine chuckles and sits beside me.

"Did you finish revising your manuscript?" she asks.

"I emailed it. Roman wants us to stay here for a long time."

"I'm so happy moving has improved your career. You're becoming even more of an international star. First in Qatar, now here."

We married a year after we met and left for Qatar a year after that, when Jasmine found a nursing post there. Our boy was born in the US before we moved out here. I've loved every bit of our lives. Finding my soulmate and living with her is better than what I'd dreamed.

"You, Olly and Baxter are the reason I've become more successful." I look over to check on Olly. He's only fifteen months old, but he can already run a few laps round the yard. "Are you sure you won't miss this wandering life when we return home next year?"

"I loved the two years we spent in Qatar, just the two of us. I'm having a ball working here but I want Olly to grow up near his grandparents and go to school in Blossom Ford. It'll be easier for him to see his cousins, too. We can always travel later, when he's in college."

I nod, full of optimism for the life ahead of us. Sometimes I get scared, however I live each day to the fullest. I call Olly and Baxter, and we head inside for Jasmine to shower and change before we go on our usual walk along the beach.

Fancy more short and steamy instalove Boxsets from Iris West? Check out Curvy Brides Of Blossom Ford Books 5-8.

FREE BOOK

WOULD YOU LIKE A free book? Sign up to my mailing list at https://dl.bookfunnel.com/t191w45ryj to receive a copy of Loving My Fake Husband, a Curvy Brides of Blossom Ford Series short story.

HELP OTHERS FIND THIS BOOK

THANK YOU FOR READING Curvy Brides Of Blossom Ford Books 1-4. If you enjoyed this book, please help others discover it by leaving a review. Many thanks,

Iris xx

ABOUT THE AUTHOR

Iris West writes short and steamy romance about alpha heroes and the women they can't help falling in love with. She loves reading all types of romance books that have a happy ending and is an avid Kdrama fan.

Follow or like her on Facebook, Goodreads, Bookbub, Tiktok,Instagram and/or Amazon.

Printed in Dunstable, United Kingdom